INTO

THEIR

STRIDE

INTO THEIR STRIDE

Lendorph & la Cour

ISBN: 978-87-4305-895-3

Cover illustration by Anne Gyrite Schütt ©

Publisher: BoD · Books on Demand GmbH, In de Tarpen 42,

22848 Norderstedt, Germany

Print: Libri Plureos GmbH, Friedensallee 273,

22763 Hamburg, Germany

Read more at

www.lendorphandlacour.com

Upcoming books in the series

A Personal Touch

Across the World

All things Hidden

Family Matters

Editor of Aftenbladet, Bærentzen, sat at his desk, tapping his fingers on the table, quite unsure if he was about to make a mistake. According to the appointment, there were only a couple of minutes left until a Miss Anna Lendorph would walk through the door as an applicant for a journalist position. A woman in a newsroom? Rasmussen would be against it, no doubt about it, but it wasn't his decision; in fact, he wasn't even told. However, Miss Lendorph had the language skills Bærentzen needed, and no men had applied on such impressive qualifications.

The sound of the front door made him look up, and there she was. Young, red-haired, elegant in a smart suit with matching hat, sharp grey-green eyes... hmm... perhaps not the worst idea after all. He rose to welcome her and asked her to sit down.

- You're an academic, I see. Not strictly necessary, but your language skills are precisely what I'm looking for. You mentioned you've been to boarding schools in both Switzerland and England?

- Yes, although only a couple of years at each place. Enough to speak French, Italian, and English fluently. German, of course, I already knew – as do most, I suppose.

- Excellent. What I need is someone capable of reading foreign newspapers and telegrams and find the right pieces for Aftenbladet's readers – and reproduce them in our style. Not translate, but write based on the information from, say, Figaro.

- I'm sure I can do that to your satisfaction.

Editor Bærentzen still looked unsure. Anna, on the other hand, was anything but. Bærentsen needed a little more to be certain.

- You know that it's primarily crime stories that catch the readers' attention – which can be a bit... gruesome?

- Of course. But I take a personal interest in crime stories – I must admit, I read both Émile Gaboriau – You know Monsieur Lecoq, I presume? – and Conan Doyle, of course. And not just because he is my great-uncle.

- You read Sherlock Holmes? And are related to Conan Doyle?

Bærentzen had a hard time hiding his enthusiasm.

- Yes. My grandmother is English and related to his mother – and perhaps soon even more – his brother is courting Clara Swendsen, who is also family. I have met him a couple of times in London and visited him at Windlesham.

That dispelled the last shred of doubt. For a former freelance crime reporter, it was the perfect bait. Conan Doyle's niece or something. Bærentzen was almost star-struck.

- Well then, I expect you to be familiar with criminology and all its challenges – and that it will be routine to describe foreign events accurately.

- Elementary.

Anna couldn't resist, even though it was silly. But the effect was the intended. The decision had been made; it was evident in the changed tone and expectant look, even though they were being suppressed. Anna noted the change with satisfaction. Her homework had paid off.

- What else do you do besides reading?

- Fencing. Pistol shooting – on a range, of course. I attend a lot of theatre and lectures, mostly scientific.

Bærentzen was impressed against his will.

- Well then. Are you engaged, Miss Lendorph?

- No. I've been busy with my education and have travelled a lot. I'm in no hurry.

That was true enough. No need to elaborate that marriage held absolutely no interest. End up as a man's personal property? No way.

- Excellent.

A sweeping gesture indicated it was time to meet the rest of the editorial staff, which as this particular time turned out to be one very disgruntled male journalist. Bærentzen and Anna went out into the newsroom – a smallish room with wood panelling, a large world map, shelves with various books, including dictionaries, stacks of used and unused notepads, and something that looked like a trophy. The general lighting was unimpressive, but there were proper lamps on the desks in the classic design – brass and green glass.

Bærentzen pointed to an empty desk with a leather chair imprinted with a bottom as padded as the chair, an older model telephone, and – evidently no expense spared – the very latest in typewriters: the best and newest Remington with key-set tabulator. There was also a tray stand and a mysterious sharp metal object that looked like a spike on a wooden block.

- This will be your desk.

Anna glanced at the other desks to see if there was anything to illuminate the function of the spike. They all had a similar contraption with paper impaled on it. To do spike or wastepaper basket? That would have to wait.

Bærentsen regained attention with an introduction to the older colleague. A middle-aged, thin-haired, bespectacled gentleman in a brown suit, a hideous tie in rusty red colours, and a musty facial expression, partially hidden behind a beard.

- Carl, this is Miss Lendorph. She'll do our foreign affairs. Miss Lendorph – journalist Carl Rasmussen. He also writes our serials under the pseudonym Jens Hammer.

Mr Rasmussen was clearly unenthusiastic, although he attempted a grimace vaguely resembling a smile. Anna smiled back and extended her hand.

- How do you do, Mr Rasmussen?

He managed a surprisingly limp handshake. Both Rasmussen and Anna were relieved that their areas of work were entirely different and did not entail cooperation of any kind.

Almost simultaneously and not far away, another conversation similar to the first was initiated. Police sergeant Christian la Cour had had a talk with his superior, police inspector Hakon Jørgensen, who had suggested he applied for the vacant position in the

Detective Office of the Copenhagen Police. Not that Jørgensen wanted rid of him, but he had abilities. At 29, he was mature enough, and for Christian, it was both a promotion and a challenge, although his time with Jørgensen had been quite extraordinary. So, now he sat in front of Assistant Commissioner of Police, Henrik Madsen, head of the Detective Office. A tall, middle-aged man with cropped, grey hair, a military style moustache, and a gaze that clearly indicated he could not be fooled.

- So, you want to be a detective?

- Yes. I believe I have the abilities. At least, that's what my inspector thinks. He was the one who brought this opportunity to my attention.

- I see... Your background is somewhat unusual?

- I have completed my military service as a guardsman, and I've been at Nørrebro police station for three years.

- Of course. But ballet?

- Yes, I've been a principal dancer. Had to leave because of an injury that would have left me disabled had I continued.

The last remark elicited a smile from the chief.

- The ballerina was too heavy? You know that a certain physical standard is expected? But I suppose you already know from Nørrebro.

- I can throw a left hook too, should I need it.

Henrik Madsen's smile turned into a chuckle:

- I didn't know one got into scuffles in the corps de ballet?

Christian grinned back:

- You'd be amazed, sir. But it was mostly outside. Being a boy attending ballet classes in my neighbourhood was tougher than being a constable.

- Yes, I can imagine. And did you develop a left-handed combat technique there?

- Let's just say, I got good at avoiding a beating and gained a certain reputation for using... lesser-known techniques...

Madsen took a closer look at his applicant. Young, tall, dark-haired, brown eyes, almost girlishly handsome and unusually well-built. And according to Jørgensen, someone the diverse clientele who occasionally took a short, involuntary break at Nørrebro Police Station had a lot of respect for. Perhaps because he could carry most of them in one arm while they struggled to touch the ground.

- Yes, you certainly seem to be in good physical shape. Anything else I should know about you?

- I'm familiar with police work in Paris and their new methods. Besides French – because of ballet – I also speak German and English.

- Indeed. Why the English?

- I learned English by reading Sherlock Holmes in the original language, and took classes because I considered going to America with Ingeborg, my former fiancée. We studied together. Then she left and I didn't.

- And now you want to be the Sherlock Holmes of Copenhagen?

Madsen couldn't resist a hint of sarcasm, even though Jørgensen had assured him that sergeant la Cour was well qualified.

- More like Monsieur Lecoq, sir. I'm used to working within the police force.

And good at speaking up for himself, Madsen had to acknowledge. He resolved to follow Jørgensen's advice.

- Excellent. We can certainly keep up as well. Our Central Bureau of Identification is greatly admired throughout Europe, and right now, we have a success rate of 100 per cent. I look forward to your contribution to raising the standard even further. Talk to Senior Inspector Schou; he will give you your new badge and a copy of the Instructions and Gross' handbook on criminal investigation, which I expect you to read as soon as possible, and which may show you that Mr Holmes isn't as unique as one might think. I assume you are well-versed in police regulations? Schou will also meet you when you start on duty and, among other things, take you to the laboratory, the museum, the Central Bureau, and to the Institute of Forensic Medicine, with whom you will collaborate.

- Of course.

- You can hand in your uniform at your station – we dress in plain clothes. A desk will be ready for you on Monday. You are now officially among the best in the police force. We expect you to perform accordingly.

Madsen watched Christian as he left the office. Poised – in a police uniform. Something didn't quite add up, but it would only be for a few more days. He would look natural in civilian attire, and – one could hope – would be fully capable of a top performance on manners and good conduct, which were the top brass' new favourite words, besides being tough, which was just as necessary even though things were changing.

Madsen remembered Jørgensen's explanation: 'He can give them a wallop and lift the rascal into the wagon with one arm, while being the picture of kindness, so they're almost thanking him for the arrest. Never seen anything like it.' That sounded promising. The challenge now was to place him. He didn't resemble any of the others and might come off as provocative to some. A bit too elegant. A bit too... different. Especially intelligent, if one were to believe Jørgensen.

For now, he decided to let him have a desk to himself with no one opposite until he could see how it went. The gossip would start immediately, no doubt about it – no one can gossip like policemen – and then he would see how la Cour handled it. And soon, there would come yet another new officer, who, apart from the intelligence, was almost his opposite. A country boy who would be just as different, only differently different. Both would need a partner. Detectives worked best in twos. They would encounter things on the job that would be easier to bear if they were two to talk. Two who knew what they had seen. But first, Schou had to take care of la Cour and get him up to speed. They would get along well, he was sure. Same with Bugge at the Central Bureau. It would all work out fine.

Christian hadn't had time to explore the surroundings when he arrived, as Madsen was punctual; it had only taken a couple of minutes before he was shown into the office. On his way out, he took a closer look at his new workplace. It was a beautiful room, with a very high ceiling, huge arched windows, fine panels, shelves, paintings, and a door leading to a corridor with a big staircase and a row of offices. It was an impressive room in an imposing building filled with expectations for the police's new department of specialised detectives and the already famous, Central Bureau of Identification.

The entire room hummed with concentration and activity. It smelled of hair pomade, leather, pencils, damp wool, furniture polish, paper, and ink, with a slight hint of tobacco, lingering in the clothing – smoking was clearly not allowed in the room.

Only the very best was working here, and now he was one of them. Christian smiled as he walked down the stairs at the back of the courthouse, where a rather inconspicuous brass plate announced that this was the entrance to the Detective Office. Detective Christian la Cour. It had a good ring to it. And Madsen didn't need to worry about how quickly he would read Gross. That book had been read long ago. It was already on the shelf at home, and Madsen was right. One could almost think Mr Holmes had read it – or rather – Conan Doyle.

1.

Anna sat at her new desk in the newsroom – still not quite accustomed to the situation – and sifted through various foreign newspapers to find stories that might interest Aftenbladet's readers.

Cambriolage de Bijoux à Bordeaux. Tiare célèbre et autres Diamants volés à MM. Roux & Calmette. La police n'a pas de pistes.

That sounded interesting – at least interesting enough for a similar spot in Aftenbladet, which generally took an interest in crime stories and celebrities, including their tiaras and assorted diamonds. Here was the story, but unfortunately, not with all the details. It would be necessary to send a telegram to Bordeaux. Why was the tiara famous? Who owned it or had owned it? It was out of the question to write anything without a name and preferably one with a title, if it was to invoke any interest in Copenhagen. Perhaps the local countess could afford a 20,000 francs tiara? The police clueless? Surely it couldn't last long – the tiara must be recognisable.

So, questions ready for Bordeaux and the final additions on today's foreign front-page story:

A tree for a house.

Gardener Jones is standing in the doorway of his abode. His horse coming out of the stables. The accompanying picture, photographed by John William Gardner, originates from Gibbsland in British Columbia, Canada, and is rather self-explanatory. Only we should mention that it is the gardener, Mr Jones, who has hollowed out the mighty tree stump and turned it into a comfortable home, as well as a stable, with room for a horse and two cows.

There had to be something amusing alongside the crime stories and war rumblings, which otherwise filled many newspapers. All newspapers. Even Aftenbladet, which was a small afternoon paper, where war wasn't the focus quite as much as in the morning papers, even though it was just as international. It was also big on photo illustrations.

Aftenbladet's readers were kept updated on everything from the coronation of the emperor in India to a young lady's escape from Gl. Kongevej. There was drama and entertainment, crime, and sensation, and plenty of advertisements. Like other newspapers, there was also a serial on Sundays. The paper had gone through a period of focusing on social indignation, but after a change in owner and editorship, the focus was now mostly on entertainment. It had had a positive effect on circulation. Editor Bærentzen had once been a freelance crime reporter and still had a weakness for crime stories. Fortunately, so did his readers.

Anna continued to leaf through the foreign papers: Le Figaro, The Times, Berliner Morgenpost... It was just fine to get paid for reading the papers, but... Maybe a desk job like this wasn't quite her thing after all? Anna read on. She had had slightly greater expectations for a job as a journalist than simply writing copy from other people's stories while sitting at a desk. It was essentially just ordinary office work, although she tried to make the most of the stories, including choosing some that required leaving the office. Her bottom might be smaller than the imprint in the inherited chair, but her intellect felt cramped in the small newsroom after just a few days. At least it was only part-time. It wasn't the money that drew her, but the opportunity to go out and experience new things.

Christian had almost settled at his desk, now cluttered with various reports, books, and case files, as he familiarised himself with the machinations of the Detective Office. He had accompanied Schou to meet Bugge, the head of the Central Bureau of Identification – it had been a good meeting, and they had hit it off immediately. The visit to the laboratory had also been useful – there he could collect supplies for the contents of his detective kit, and it was nice to speak to people who had professional expertise with the materials he expected to use – and which, to his great surprise, no one else seemed to know about. It had been different at the Forensic Institute, but it was also more of a hospital than a police facility.

He compared the cases he had seen and the people he had met until he could spot the connections, and Schou's explanations both in the field and in the office were precise and made sense. He knew Gross inside out, so he felt reasonably prepared to get involved in a fresh case.

Christian shifted restlessly in the rather uncomfortable wooden chair, which didn't quite fit in height, and scanned the room full of new colleagues. He was used to being around many people, but not that many new ones at once. He could remember some names, but far from all of them. The atmosphere was industrious, although there were clearly friendships among some men. There just wasn't much time to get to know anyone, and he felt alien and different – scrutinised without quite knowing why.

No more time for philosophising. Madsen came out of his office and went straight for Christian's desk.

- La Cour?

- Yes?

- You're off to Kronprinsensgade 11. And I think you'll need everything Jørgensen taught you.

That sounded a lot better than reading old case files, and Christian straightened his back and sat almost to attention as Madsen went on:

- Break-in at Møinichen's jewellery shop – from above. You're to examine the crime scene, both floors. Mrs Jensen, the caretaker's wife, discovered the break-in at half-past five this morning. Make sure no one touches anything. I'll take care of Møinichen. He's in the country. His assistant will come at nine and must not enter the premises until we're finished.

- Very well. I'll go straight away.

Finally, a chance to test his talents – and in particular the new detective kit, which Jørgensen had explained about for more than an hour at one of the new police courses, and which now contained everything Jørgensen had written on the blackboard plus various items Christian himself had added after reading Gross's book: Pocket camera, white, report, concept, tissue, blotting and tracing paper, special cards, pencils, pen and ink, ruler, pedometer, footprint gauge, a box of wax, a bottle of dry plaster of Paris, a can of Vaseline, varnish, torch, compass, magnifying glass, a small bottle of rubber solution with brush in the lid, a small bottle of glue with brush in the lid, a sable brush, a small tin of carbon dust, sailmaker's twine, chalk, glass phials with cork stoppers, pocket handkerchiefs, tweezers, envelopes, small brown paper bags, larger paper bags, a large cloth bag, a pair of thin silk gloves and a pair of kid gloves.

The bag was the size and shape of a doctor's bag, made of brown leather with a few large compartments and several small ones. It had taken some time to find a bag that suited the purpose – large enough and with enough compartments, but it still had to be adapted. Perhaps that was why the others were looking at him like that. There certainly weren't any others who had a bag like it, even though some of them had attended the same Police Association's evening class.

Gross's handbook – and Jørgensen's lessons – were embossed on his mind, so he could almost rifle through them with an index and everything in his memory. Learning and remembering. Some things are sharpened with practice, and as a dancer, the ability to learn and remember is essential. You're either good or you're out, and no one would be in any doubt. He had leafed through many pages in his head when he turned the corner into Kronprinsensgade.

Møinichen's establishment was situated at the end of the street in a large building on the corner of Pilestræde. It was renowned for a vast selection of elegant jewellery, where one could also have heirlooms altered to meet current fashions.

Both Møinichen and his assistant had a knack for customer service, and one could be assured of sound advice regarding what would complement various hairstyles, formal attire, and assorted decorations. Or one could very gently be introduced to the discreet rules about when to wear what throughout the day and at which social functions, if one were new to wealth and wise enough to inquire. There were quite a few women and some men in Copenhagen's upper echelons who had avoided more than one embarrassing faux pas thanks to Møinichen's friendly expertise.

Christian crossed the street to get an impression of the whole place. An older but well-maintained three-storey building in red brick with sandstone cornices and an entrance to the main staircase in a gateway large enough for a carriage. There were shops on the ground floor and in the basement, offices, and flats on the first floor, and flats above.

At first glance, there was nothing to see. There were still bars across Møinichen's windows and door, but on the floor above, where there should have been curtains, cardboard boxes had been stacked in front of the windows, blocking the view. Christian went back across the street to the shop, where a closer inspection revealed that the windows were entirely bereft of jewellery. There wasn't so much as a scratch on the door or bars, so no attempted break-in that way. Christian nearly banged his forehead against the bars, trying to peer inside.

On the floor inside the shop, a stepladder was left in the middle, and beside it lay an open umbrella filled with what looked like construction debris. He looked up. Directly above the stepladder was a hole in the ceiling, large enough for a smaller person to fit through. Easy to see how the thieves had got in. And no doubt they had taken everything of value. The shop had been emptied of goods – only one display case appeared untouched, twinkling in colourful solitude in the grey morning light.

Christian entered through the gateway, where a local policeman stood guard at the door.

- Detective Sergeant La Cour – has anyone been here since the thieves and Mrs Jensen?

- Constable Nielsen. No. Noone.

- Good.

The stairwell resembled other stairwells in the neighbourhood – broad, with wooden panels and painted plaster imitating decorations from Pompeii, wrought-iron railings with a polished handrail of dark wood; well-kept and without any useful marks on the steps. There was a faint smell of brown soap with a hint of cigar smoke. The door to the shop was still locked, and there were no signs of any attempted break-in, so Christian proceeded to the first floor, where the door was ajar. A brass sign announced that the current tenants were Rasmussen & Dahl.

Christian opened the door fully by pushing it with a finger.

The room was dimly lit and dusty, and you could just make out footprints in the dust on the floor. Christian stood in the doorway, put his bag down and his gloves on and felt for light switches by the inside doorframe. They were where expected.

Christian switched on the ceiling lights, which were quite bright, so there must have been enough light to work, if they had been on. They probably had been, as boxes and crates were stacked in front of the windows to prevent anyone from noticing the light, if they had thought to look up from the street.

First, photos – door, inside, footprints... camera away and grabbing the chequered paper Christian crouched down to measure and draw. Christian's nose also went to work. There was a smell of mustiness, dust, paper, and... cheap cigars? Very faintly, so there couldn't have been anyone smoking in the room, but perhaps the smell clung to the clothes, or it had been lingering for a long time? Certainly, no ashtrays in sight.

Christian put a couple of the small boxes into a paper bag for Bugge. He examined the larger ones. 'If I were to lift one like this, I'd hold it here and here.' Dusting with carbon powder revealed that the thieves had done just that. There were marks on the corners, but nothing that could be of use.

A further look around the room didn't reveal much and certainly no goods or office work of any kind – tables and shelves were empty. Rasmussen and Dahl couldn't have been around recently. But there was a disturbance in the dust on one of the tables; someone must have left something here. Something large – perhaps a bag, and something that had left marks in the dust. Tools of some sort? It was impossible to tell.

Christian moved some boxes to let more daylight into the room. He walked cautiously around, trying to look at the floors and walls from different angles. There was nothing useful; someone had been walking around moving things, and all traces crossed each other in one big mess. The only marks that stood out were by a wall and could have been made by the stepladder, which had prevented the dust from settling for quite some time.

Around the hole in the floor, there were traces of a lot of activity. Christian tried to read them. The outermost ones could have been made by tools laid behind someone's back. He took photos and moved closer, squatting down with his coat wedged between his legs so as not to leave new marks, and tried to imagine what had happened. What do you do if you need to drill holes in a floor? You kneel. That would fit. Perhaps three people who had moved sideways around the hole. It matched well with the drilling work, where the holes weren't uniform. Streaks in the dust could suggest they had worn long coats. Tools had been put as far back as one could reach while kneeling. There were a lot of splinters and drill bits – you couldn't have got a saw directly into the gap, which had been filled with clay.

Christian took a series of photos, as he would need to get closer to the hole to examine it properly, and that would mean he would mess up the traces. He went right up to the edge and squatted down again.

The edge was jagged. Torch and magnifying glass revealed threads embedded in the splintered wood. Christian took his tweezers and carefully extracted the threads, placing them in an envelope.

The hole was between two of the load-bearing beams, so it wasn't very large – one thief must have been very slender.

Christian tried to imagine how one would get down. But first, the stepladder must have been lowered down and set up. And the umbrella? It must have been held open under the hole while they worked. Probably so that the falling plaster and clay wouldn't make a lot of noise. So, someone must have held the umbrella while the others punched through the fill between the floors and the ceiling below. Here, the thieves had been lucky – straw and clay and underneath only boards almost as thin as cardboard as base for the plaster ceiling.

Had the thieves been lucky, or had they known? The age of the house was an indication. They had certainly expected it, since they had brought an umbrella. It hadn't rained, so it wasn't a coincidence.

Someone had thought ahead. Merde!

Constable Nielsen suddenly appeared in the doorway.

- La Cour? The clerk has arrived.
- I'm coming down.

Christian took off his gloves and grabbed his bag. Outside the door stood a younger man, hat in hand and with an anxious expression.

- I need to open the shop?

Christian offered his hand with a reassuring smile.

- Detective Christian La Cour. I'll come down with you – and in.

The clerk, Søren Svendsen, fumbled a bit with the keys. There were three solid locks on the door. In the back room, there was no sign of activity. No footprints, no marks on the safe – the thieves apparently hadn't even been in the room. How very odd.

- What's in the safe?

- Contracts, accounts, customer lists, inventories, loose stones, gold, unfinished work, jewellery waiting for alterations...

- And the doors are locked, as they should be, I see – both here and on the street. You're not needed here right now, but if you come back – let's say at two o'clock – you can make a list of the missing jewellery when we're done her?

The relieved clerk hurried out, but then pivoted on his heel and came back.

- What about the keys? Should I give them to you?

- Yes, please. I don't know if we'll be done before two, but then at least we can lock up until we come back.

The clerk left, and it was time to inspect the goods. Or rather – the abundant lack thereof. Just one display case had not been touched, even though it twinkled invitingly with multi-coloured stones. Glass? Rhine-stones? Obviously, nothing of interest, for there wasn't so much as a fingerprint on the glass. The other display cases were open but not damaged and emptied of contents except for minor items, which would probably turn out to be of no significance. No footprints; the shop had been properly cleaned, so the only dust in the room was what had come down during the break-in. In this there were lots of footprints, but they looked odd and were all on top of each other and totally useless. Christian took photos of the room, display cases, dust... and then there was the umbrella. Gloves back on – maybe fingerprints on the handle? Bugge had better take care of those, if there were any. The umbrella was filled with dust, clay, plaster, straw, and... Christian fished out a worn, knitted sock foot. The cause of the strange footprints? It went into a bag together with some clumps of plaster and clay. He left the umbrella. It would need to be emptied before it could be moved, and others would have to take care of that. So, professional thieves, who knew how to be quiet, and who had come in and out without anyone hearing or seeing anything. Probably with a huge haul. Christian took off his gloves and put them in the bag. He locked up to go straight to Bugge at the Central Bureau of Identification. As he came out of the gate, he was interrupted by a man from the Mende hardware store in the basement right under Møinichen's.

- What happened?
- Who are you?

- Lars Christian Andersen, clerk at Mende.

- Detective La Cour. There's been a burglary at Møinichen's.

- Thought as much. Just yesterday, Niels and I were talking about it.

- Why?

- There were a couple of strange blokes sniffing around here a few days ago.

He turned and shouted down,

- Niels – come up here, will ya?

His colleague put down a barrel and came up to the street.

- You remember those two lurking around?

- The two who looked like English footballers?

- Yeah. They were traipsing about here – kept going back and forth and staring at this building. Walked past each other as if strangers and then a little later, they came back the other way and talked while they kept staring. We thought they were so odd; we wrote it down. Wait a min...

Lars Andersen went into the shop and fetched a piece of paper.

- You can have this. One tall, dark, foreign-looking, about 20 years old, the other quite small, also dark. Same age. Very elegantly dressed.

Christian took the paper and put it in his bag.

- Thank you very much, gentlemen. That was very observant of you. Perhaps of crucial importance.

He tipped his hat and left, while the two shop assistants patted each other on the back and continued their work in the shop. Christian went straight to Bugge.

Bugge looked sympathetically at the latest addition to the Detective Office. A man after his own heart. Precise, meticulous, systematic... may the next additions to the force be like him.

- La Cour! What do you bring?

Bugge looked expectantly at Christian.

- Kronprinsensgade. Photographs, threads, prints, a description of two mysterious men... and a sock foot.

- A sock foot??

Christian carefully took the various items out of the bag and laid them next to each other on the long counter. All carefully labelled with content and location of discovery and sketched on a diagram of both the first floor and the shop. Bugge looked at the collection and sketches and nodded approvingly.

- By the book. I like that.

- I also have photographs. Will you develop them here?

- Of course. What did it look like?

Christian explained the scene in detail.

- And precision work all the way through, although I don't understand the part about the sock foot. One would rather expect jewel thieves to be able afford real socks?

Bugge chuckled and lifted it up with a large pair of tweezers to inspect it with a magnifying glass.

- Wool – and judging by the button, Danish. Skin flakes, wear, holes, repairs but no traces of insects. No eggs, no lice, no lost wings.

Bugge sniffed it.

- And someone has definitely worn it. For a long time.

Bugge handed it to Christian, who cautiously sniffed it and then wrinkled his nose.

- I suppose.

- I'll process the items, develop the photographs, check for prints, and call you when I have something to report unless you want me over now?

- Please, and yes, preferably now. The assistant should be allowed in to record what's been stolen; he'll be back at two, so we should ideally be finished before then.

Bugge nodded. He had already decided to go to Kronprinsensgade himself to secure the last clues from things that couldn't be moved, and like the fingerprints on the edge of the hole and the umbrella – were difficult to deal with unless one happened to have special equipment. Christian had filled the counter, so it was unlikely there was more to find except said umbrella, whose contents would need to be sifted just in case. Bugge's sympathy was growing. 'He takes what he can and leaves what he can't. And he can tell the difference. How lucky can one be that he ended up with Jørgensen, who is sharper than Sherlock and could see the talent –

and had the decency to hand him over to Madsen. He even knows Gross's handbook by heart. Perhaps one should thank the higher powers some time.'

As expected, Bugge was right. There was nothing more to find except the umbrella and the fingerprints at the hole, so the clerk was allowed to clean up and start on his very long list of stolen goods. It would take days to cross-reference through the books to make sure the list was correct.

2.

Bærentzen, owner and editor of Aftenbladet, stood with his coat on and hat in hand in his large office, hanging up the phone. It was beneficial to have connections in the police force when something happened, and this was front-page material. And very bad timing. There was no excuse for missing a family funeral – heist or no heist – so... 'but couldn't those damn burglars have waited until tonight instead?' Bærentzen had a good relationship with the Detective Office, where he had known the Assistant Commissioner, Henrik Madsen, for several years from his time as a freelance crime reporter. He had distinguished himself by writing what had actually happened, without fanciful embellishments. Catchy headlines but no guesswork or sensational nonsense. At Aftenbladet, there was always room for notices on both items and people, and whatever else the police felt the need to share with the public. That meant he often got the news first, and he carefully made sure they didn't regret it. Journalism was about reality – fiction was Rasmussen's domain under the pseudonym Hammer. On Sundays.

Bærentzen entered the newsroom, where Rasmussen was absent. Entirely understandable – he had enough to do, and the prospect of Anna had shifted his activities, which did not involve work at the typewriter, to relocate to the nearest pub. A female colleague was an insult he didn't want up close, if there were any alternatives. Especially not if the alternatives involved coffee, he didn't have to make himself, and alcohol served by the bottle. Rasmussen's presence in the newsroom had become extremely sparse, but Bærentzen had no intention of reprimanding him, as long as his articles maintained the usual standard and were delivered on time.

'One can only hope that the kinship with Doyle has rubbed off', thought Bærentzen as he looked at Anna, who glanced up from the typewriter as he emerged from his office.

- 45,000 – jewellery worth 45,000! One could say it's worth the trouble.

Anna looked questioningly at Bærentzen.

- Burglary in Kronprinsensgade – and not a scratch on neither door nor windows.

- Sounds professional. I assume you're heading to the Detective Office to get more details?

- Well, yes, under normal circumstances I would be, but I am otherwise engaged today. Uh...

- Shall I go?

Anna was on the verge of beaming, but managed to maintain a professionally expectant look.

- Are you sure you are up to it?

- Completely sure. Is there someone you usually speak to I should ask for – and I'll be off right away?

- Yes. I usually speak with Henrik Madsen – but he's not always there. If not, ask for whoever is handling the case. Prepare an article for early tomorrow. Front page. I must leave and won't be back today.

- Of course.

Bærentzen was barely out of the office before Anna allowed herself to cheer. A different day. A completely different day. Going out to actually do something. Finally. Hat, coat, gloves, bag – here I come! Anna practically flew out the door. She walked from Lande-mærket to Nytorv and the Courthouse with the Detective Office and a reception manned by an aging character with a handlebar moustache and an elevator gaze. At least when it came to female visitors. He finally lifted his eyes from their resting place on Anna's bosom.

- My name is Anna Lendorph. I am a journalist with Aftenbladet and would like to speak to Assistant Commissioner, Henrik Madsen, about the jewellery theft in Kronprinsensgade.

- I'm sorry, he's not here, Miss Lendorph.

- Can I speak with the detective in charge of the case then?

- Hmm. Wait a moment, please.

Anna looked around the large, elegant room, desks standing two by two facing each other. They filled the entire room. There was a wide door leading to a spacious hallway, where one could see offices – including Madsen's. The door was open, and the office was visibly empty. There were officers at about half the desks; all in plain clothes, and only a few had looked up when the door opened. They all looked like any other men except for a preference for moustaches, which was above average. In a corner by a window sat a younger man with no facial hair, who looked more like a film star than a police officer. Anna's gaze lingered. The desk clerk went over to the 'film star', who turned out to be wearing a midnight blue suit in a cut so modern, one would have to be a connoisseur to catch the exclusive details, a silk tie in colours shaded from blue to emerald with a glimpse of copper, and equally fashionable dark brown Oxford shoes. Gold fob – no jewellery. Anna was impressed, but also rather puzzled. It didn't look like clothes one could afford on a policeman's salary. Christian came along to the counter, where he exchanged a look with the desk clerk, very clearly indicating that his help was no longer required. Christian turned to Anna and looked her directly in the eyes without veering off to other body parts. Highly unusual. In a split second, it dawned on both that behind the other's very professional facade lurked a solid sense of humour – probably with a dark edge. Christian extended his hand.

- Detective Christian la Cour. You asked for me?

- Yes. My name is Anna Lendorph. I am a journalist at Aftenbladet and would like to hear more about the jewellery theft in Kronprinsensgade.

Christian smiled warmly.

- Of course. I am on my way there. Would you care to join me?

It was evidently not customary, as the desk clerk, who had been listening without pretending to do otherwise, looked very surprised.

- Just a moment.

Christian went back to his desk to retrieve hat and coat; a cashmere fedora in a blue-grey shade and a matching Inverness cape coat; just like the hat, with a taffeta lining changing from dark blue to emerald like the tie. Anna herself wore a dark blue winter coat with a Persian collar, a dove blue suit in Irish wool with darker blue velvet trims, matching blue handbag, and a dark blue trilby with a small velvet cockade. Small gold earrings – no wedding ring and no engagement ring either; there were no telltale bulges in the kid gloves. Discreet, practical elegance, noted Christian. And unmarried and not engaged either. Christian was one of the few who also noticed the unusual, deep pleats in the skirt, which provided extra but certainly not conspicuous freedom of movement. He judged she would be able to both run and kick, which was normally impossible for women wearing the fashion of the time. So not just tailored but to unusual specifications. Prepared for anything, apparently. Interesting.

Christian made it back to the counter, where he passed and intentionally came very close to Anna without touching, gently inhaling her scent. No cigarette smoke in the hair. Unusual for a journalist. French perfume. Jicky from Guerlain, if he wasn't mistaken. Interesting choice – daring, to say the least. Just as unusual as the pleats in the skirt. And familiar. He smiled inwardly. Christian indicated with a gesture that they should go outside, and gallantly offered his arm as they descended the stairs.

- Forgive my curiosity, but it's usually the editor himself who comes by. I didn't think there were others who wrote about crime?

- I write the foreign news which also contains quite a lot of crime stories, so it's not new to me.

They crossed Nytorv diagonally, as directly as possible, between all the stalls. Christian was still curious. He had never met a female journalist before, and Bærentzen was not someone he thought would delegate a good robbery. He attempted some polite conversation. Perhaps it was possible to solve this little mystery?

- Are you interested in crime stories?

- Absolutely. Maybe there's not so much difference between being a journalist and a detective.

Christian thought it was a bit thick, but male journalists rarely lacked in confidence – especially not said editor Bærentzen – so maybe women journalists were the same? Both the suit and perfume suggested the wearer couldn't be entirely ordinary.

- How so?

- It's about finding the core of the story, where 'every little detail can be crucial.'

Christian recognised the quote from one of his favourite books and brightened up.

- Monsieur Lecoq!

- Bien sûr.

Some friendships arise in an instant and require no great buildup. For example, when you discover that the person, you're talking to is the only other person you've ever met who knows your favourite book. For both Anna and Christian, it was a bit of a revelation that they weren't entirely alone in loving an obscure French detective. It also made everything much easier. Christian expected – quite reasonably – that Anna had never read Gross' fantastic handbook on detective work, but she couldn't be completely clueless if she knew Lecoq. And since he was mostly used to communicating in technical terms, it would make things easier when they arrived at the crime scene, where under normal circumstances civilians – and especially women – would never ever be allowed in.

Anna hoped she could keep up when she would soon see a real crime scene – without blood, you can't have it all – and not sound like, 'women don't know anything about anything,' which was just about the worst thing that could possibly happen to her – including being run over by a tram wearing torn and/or dirty underwear and/or stockings, which was otherwise the very worst catastrophe that could befall a woman according to her grandmother. The concern would normally be with no basis, which also turned out to be the case now. Partly because she could keep up just fine, and partly because Christian didn't treat her like 'a woman' – i.e., tried to simplify things so her poor little brain wouldn't overheat from all that information. Something some doctors still used as an argument against women's suffrage or access to higher education. It felt fantastic but also very unfamiliar.

In the shop Møinichen's clerk sat trying to make a list of the missing items, with books scattered over the large worktable. Christian introduced Anna only as Miss Lendorph, knowing full well that the word 'journalist' would hardly be met with enthusiasm. They went upstairs, where the lock had not yet been repaired, and the room was empty and quiet enough to show and explain. It was an instructive hour for Anna, who was shown all the details with explanations – the marks at the lock, the footprints, the dustless spots where the stepladder had stood, where the fabric threads had stuck, the presumed size of the drills used, the marks on the table, how one could tell something about the thickness of the coats the thieves had worn from the traces on the floor, where they had knelt – and about the stepladder and umbrella, which were now removed, and where the thief had held onto the floor on the way down. Concise and methodical in the order, Christian was convinced the thieves had worked. It was like having the plot of a film explained. She could picture it. Anna was thrilled. Apparently, you could read a room the same as you could read a book. Or a dinner party. That was more her turf, but the workings were the same. A lot of small details, which together gave a picture of what had happened – and with the dinner party, were still happening and quite possibly with a chance to predict the future. And it was certainly right up there with Lecoq. Even the smallest detail... Anna understood why Bærentzen kept such things to himself. It was fun. Challenging. Fascinating. 'I want more', she said to herself, pondering how this could be achieved. Anna looked around from door to windows to hole...

- How long has all this taken?

- Hard to say. Depends on how many there were. I guess three judging by the marks, so more than an hour, but probably less than two. It all gives the impression that they've done it before – it hasn't taken longer than absolutely necessary – drilling takes as long as it takes – and they haven't hurried so much, they've caused extra problems for themselves. And they've been really lucky with the floor. It simply couldn't have been easier. My guess is that it's an international gang of thieves. I think I've read about similar thefts abroad; I just can't remember where.

Anna suddenly saw light at the end of the tunnel. Tomorrow, she had to hand in her article, and Bærent-zen would surely take over the case again, but if it was international, then there was at least a chance, just a tiny chance, that the next days wouldn't end in time as thick as treacle while Bærentzen enjoyed himself with the jewellery theft.

- Let's go downstairs.

They went down, past the clerk who was struggling with the list of stolen goods, and out into the shop where the display cases stood empty – except for one, which sparkled invitingly in the sunlight. Anna went over to the display case and pointed.

- Why haven't they taken these?

- It's silver, gilt, paste, rhinestones. Worthless compared to gold and diamonds, and probably not something the thieves' clients would touch. Easy enough to flog, but it's a different clientele. If the door to the street had been broken open, others would most likely have taken the opportunity and helped themselves to the rest – where some of it could already be on it's third owner. It doesn't go quite as fast with the expensive items, but I'll find out if anything comes on the market.

- How?

- I know people I can ask.

Christian thought of Helena, among others, but she was not someone to mention to Miss Lendorph. She might get quite the wrong impression, and Helena shouldn't be subjected to journalistic interest either.

- Have you seen what you needed, Miss Lendorph?

- Yes. Thank you. Yes, I had better go back to the newsroom and write. And thank you very much for the tour. It gives a completely different understanding when you've seen the place and had an explanation.

- Let me know if I can help you further.

Christian bowed slightly, tipped his hat, and went back to the Courthouse, where a lot of report writing awaited him as well as replenishing his detective bag. Miss Lendorph had been an experience. Quick, sharp, attentive, focused. Interesting. She reminded him of both Ingeborg and Helena.

Anna returned to the newsroom, while trying to write in her mind. When she reached the typewriter, there was enough clarity for an article that almost wrote itself.

At dinner in the Lendorph household at Kronprinsesse-gade, there were no shortage of topics of conversation – Anna delivered a full account of her first assignment as a real journalist, and Anna's mother smiled intermittently in a way Anna found very annoying, which she promptly pointed out when her father retired to his library to read.

- What's with all the sideways glances?

Dr Agnes Lendorph tilted her head and looked at her very independent and authoritative 27-year-old daughter, who generally could scare the life out of most people – especially young men – and then said very casually, as casually as possible when there's a whole queue of ulterior motives:

- Tell me a bit more about that detective.

And she thought, perhaps there was hope for Anna after all, since she blushed and he clearly hadn't been scared – quite the opposite. It warmed a mother's heart. But maybe she shouldn't put too much pressure on right now. It had proven to backfire before.

- There's not much else to say. He looks like a film star, moves like a panther, knows what he's talking about, and can speak French. Otherwise, he wouldn't be able to read Lecoq. And tomorrow, Bærentzen is back, so that's probably the last I've seen of him, and therefore, of no importance.

'Let's see,' thought Agnes, who knew Anna's voice down to the last hertz, and perhaps something could be done about it, and something would be done, no matter the cost. So, she smiled sweetly at her daughter and called for Marie, who immediately came and cleared the table. And otherwise, one might lend a helping hand. Anna didn't inherit her attention or inventiveness from strangers. Unfortunately, her determination seemed more directed towards playing the detective herself rather than playing with one. Being patient would be a trial.

At the la Cour family home on Linnés Plads, where Christian was visiting, he told his mother, former ballerina and later chorus dancer, Ida la Cour, about his day's work. It didn't escape mother Ida's attention either that her son had a little more on his mind than catching thieves.

- Tell a bit more about that journalist. Do you usually invite them to a crime scene?

It had roughly the same effect as Agnes's question and was delivered with the same apparent innocence and overload of ulterior motives. Christian didn't just blush a little, but lit up like a candle in the night.

- She's read Lecoq!
- And?

- Um. She's pretty, quick-witted, elegant, speaks French...

- And will she come back as the case develops?

- No. She probably won't. It's usually Bærentzen himself who calls. I don't know why it wasn't him today, but unless he's gone for a long time, he'll show up tomorrow to hear more. He usually comes by every day if there's something interesting going on. I've never seen Miss Lendorph before. She writes the foreign news.

- And how are things?

Christian looked down at his plate, which he had emptied for the second time.

- Same as usual. They stare, and I feel left out and different, and... I'm used to having to fight for position and be the best, otherwise you get the sack. There's competition here too, but it's gossip and cliques, and it's worse than at the station. Worse even than at the theatre, and I don't know the rules of the game.

- You'll learn soon enough, and you'll cope.

Ida patted her son on the back. It can be tough starting at a new job – whether as a detective or a chorus girl. But you learn, and the foreignness fades, and usually something happens to make things fall into place. But it wouldn't hurt to have a lady friend to divert the thoughts for a while.

It should be easy, but with Christian, it just wasn't. He had no trouble getting along with women, treated them as equals, wasn't shy or handsy, but he wanted a challenge, and when women were told to hide every trace of intelligence not to challenge potential suitors, it could be more than troublesome. Ingeborg had challenged him just enough, but unfortunately, the engagement hadn't lasted longer than to Vestre Pier and the steamer to America. She wondered for a second how Ingeborg and her parents were doing in New York. And now this Miss Lendorph had turned up with all the right qualifications but unfortunately with the prospect of disappearing again as quickly as a summer shower. Ida decided to find out who she was and if she could be of assistance in the matter. There definitely was a need for a distracting lady.

Later that evening, Christian visited a lady his mother had never heard of, named Helena, who made a good living by being extremely distracting to men. Christian wasn't one of them, because when they first met, she was curled up, beaten black and blue with a broken arm and ribs, blood all over her face, and a man's hands around her neck. A problem Christian had solved quickly and efficiently. The assailant ended up in prison, and Christian had visited Helena a few days later to see how she was doing. He had found a doctor and subsequently a pharmacy and done some shopping, and Helena had received treatment, and something to eat, and since then, they had been friends. They met regularly to chat about this and that, including the latest news from pubs and back alleys and associated activities, and most recently, some of the city's high-fliers' various dealings. Helena had recovered quickly, and her establishment was now among the city's most exclusive.

Right now, the conversation revolved around the possibility of some new jewellery appearing on the market, and it would be interesting to hear from whom and where if it did. But for once, something distracted Helena herself, whose attention – especially when it came to men and their moods and needs – was tuned to ultimate precision. There was a tiny change in the signal from Christian.

- You're different. Have you met a girl?
- Not like that. At work.
- It's more than work. Do you need some?
Christian chuckled.

- It's probably too early to guess. It's work. She's a journalist and was supposed to write about the break-in. And I'm sure her boss will take over tomorrow – it's his territory.

- You'll see her again. I can smell it on you.

There was a light knock on the door. Helena gave Christian a hug, enveloping him in a cloud of Jicky.

- Work calls.

And so, Christian walked home to his room in Vestergade, where, unlike all the other lodgers, he had a key to the front door, because a police officer must work round the clock, and such a lodger is a comfort to an elderly lady with a boarding house. Christian wondered if his special treatment might also include lady guests. Probably not. Mrs Berg was religious.

Could it be a coincidence that Helena and Anna had chosen the same scent? What else could they have in common? Humour – he was sure of it, even though he had only seen it as a shadow for the teensiest moment. It just wasn't likely that he would ever get to experience it. There would be a Bærentzen in the way. Two meters and 150 kilos of Bærentzen. Merde!

The next morning at the office, Bærentzen sat with coffee and rolls and read through Anna's article. It was damn good. He corrected a sentence for the look of it and expressed his satisfaction. As expected, he then declared that he would now take over the case himself, so everything was back to normal. Merde!

And thus, shortly afterwards, Bærentzen arrived at the reception at the Detective Office in the usual manner, looked around and saw Madsen's empty office and Christian at his desk. Christian was summoned to the counter, trying very hard to find a fitting face on the way. Bærentzen was fine – Christian had appreciated his extensive knowledge, enthusiasm, and precise reports, but he wasn't Miss Lendorph. And although Christian had found the right facial expression – a well-adjusted, accommodating smile – as he reached the counter, the shifting of his face on the way over had not escaped Bærentzen's attention, and it caused his own to adapt a very suggestive twinkle in the eye.

- La Cour. With all due respect – were you expecting someone else?

The accommodating smile remained in front of Christian's face, although one might think the elastic had snapped and it was floating freely in the air.

- No, of course not. We usually meet when there's something interesting to write about.

Bærentzen refrained from saying 'nice try'.

- Any progress?

- Not since yesterday, no.

- Well, then I won't keep you. Thank you very much.

Bærentzen smiled, lifted his hat politely, turned around, and left the office with a more than usual smug grin, while Christian watched him with an expression of a child who has had all his candy stolen. It was lucky for him he had his back to his colleagues and managed to put on a neutral face before they could follow his path back to his desk. Merde alors!

Back at his office, Bærentzen looked at Anna's article again – it really was perfect – and made an unusual decision. It stung a bit, but sometimes it's more fun to set the game in motion than just watch and write about it, and he had other things to do right now. Like managing his mother's estate according to her will, which would surely be both bothersome and lengthy and therefore not very compatible with what could become an equally lengthy and complicated but regrettably bloodless criminal case.

- Lendorph – come in here.

Anna saw the article lying on his desk and was momentarily worried, until she saw Bærentzen's face, which clearly showed that he was up to something, and it wasn't criticism.

- Detective la Cour seemed very disappointed when I arrived. Perhaps I should let you follow the case through? You seem to have... a good rapport...?

Bærentzen savoured the words like the connoisseur that he was, and Anna blushed slightly, but quickly regained her composure.

- I would, of course, like to follow the case all the way. It's most likely an international gang – at least that's what the police think, so it's probably my area too?

- International. Exactly. Your area. ...Actually, the method could resemble... was it Nice?

Bærentzen gave Anna a look that could have flustered a statue, but Anna had practice from her mother, so she kept a straight face.

- Yes, exactly. Nice. I'll take another look at that case – maybe we can come up with a lead?

- Excellent. I'm leaving the case in safe hands. But do remember the other foreign matters.

- Of course.

Unfortunately, Bærentzen had just been to the Detective Office, so no excuse for going there again today. It would have to be a follow-up on Nice instead. There had been a break-in; they had come in from above, but there was apparently no umbrella. So not quite the same, but the French newspapers' details didn't focus on the technical details of the burglary. It didn't make one any the wiser. In Belgium, there had

44

also been a jewel theft – value 30,000 francs – but it turned out to be a light-fingered chambermaid who had helped herself to the contents of a countess's jewellery box. A nice brief note for the paper, but not particularly interesting and not something that did anything for Anna's newfound interest in detective work.

For Christian, the day began with a visit to a cafe. A gentleman from Automat Caféen on Købmagergade had called about some suspicious guests, whose description matched the one Mr L. C. Andersen of Mende's in Kronprinsensgade had given of some men who had been observed showing prolonged interest in the building. The observant staff at the cafe turned out to be dishwasher Einar Christian Madsen and waiter Carl Hansen, both of whom had noticed the two mysterious men and were now practically tripping over each other in eagerness to explain.

Two men, speaking German, came in almost every day and always sat together at the same table by the window, reading piles of letters and drinking expensive wine. One tall and one short, in black clothes with handsome vests and hats. Very elegant. And chatty. The waiters had had the time, as the men came outside the busy hours and stayed long enough for an undisturbed chat. They were wine merchants; they had explained, and their father was a trader at the stock exchange in Hamburg, which might explain their ample funds and extensive consumption of wine, and now they were starting a business in Copenhagen.

The tall one hadn't been seen in the past three days, but the short one had been there yesterday and had mentioned that his brother had returned to Hamburg – something about a girl he'd got up the duff. And the short one was also going to Hamburg – the reason for this hadn't come up in the conversation. The only thing the waiter hadn't been told was the men's names, and he hadn't been close enough to read the names on the envelopes. A napkin was placed over the letters as soon as anyone approached the table.

Christian took notes and was shown the table with a good view of a large section of Købmagergade but not of Kronprinsensgade. One could also keep an eye on both the door and the room. He thanked them for the information and naturally asked that if they saw the gentlemen again, would they please call, and call as soon as the men stepped through the door?

Subsequently, Christian had a conversation with Madsen about whether it would be relevant to send a man to the main post office to take a closer look at people collecting poste restante. It would require permission from above – both for surveillance and for any potential confiscation of mail. Later in the day, Madsen emerged from his office and approached Christian.

- Schou has spoken to the postmaster, who says they've noticed two men collecting poste restante almost every day. Dark-haired – one 'southern looking'.

The letters are addressed to an L. Kemputt or Kemprer or something similar and a name — possibly with a B — and from Hamburg. I'm sending Jacobsen over — he's one of the few who can look inconspicuous, and has sufficient control of his bladder.

A new day at the office meant a new day with the chance of visiting the Detective Office, so at a time that was almost embarrassingly early, journalist Miss Anna Lendorph appeared at the reception after ensuring that the door made as much noise as possible. It had the desired effect. Detective la Cour reached the counter from his desk before the duty officer even had a chance to look up from his logbook.

- Miss Lendorph!

- I've just come to ask if there's anything new about the jewel theft?

An inquiry that, judging by the rapid changes in his face, caused jubilation, concern, and some quick thinking. The counter at the Detective Office was unfortunately within earshot of at least 6-8 officers. A conclusion Anna also quickly reached and worried about.

- Maybe you'd like to see... Just a moment.

Christian hurried back to his desk, put some papers in his bag, grabbed his coat and hat, and returned with a gesture towards the door.

- Please?

Anna and Christian left the Detective Office followed by smug grins and glances and – what Christian couldn't know – a much easier life at the office, where certain words and assumptions disappeared from the hushed conversations.

The rushed exit meant Christian had to put the bag on the stairs to put on his hat and coat. Not a very elegant solution, but Miss Lendorph just stood there smiling, as if it were the most natural thing in the world. 'Where can you take a lady at breakfast time?' Christian had no doubt. La Glace, where the owner, Anina, could surely serve coffee and croissants to accompany a conversation about mysterious men at Automat Caféen.

Anina found a table at the back and immediately brought coffee.

- Croissants?

- Yes, please, thank you.

Anna took out her notebook, and Christian a stack of notes, and both immediately realised that cafe tables were too small if there were also to be cups and plates on the table. It was cumbersome to manoeuvre, and you felt watched by the others in the cafe and even by yourself, as you caught glimpses of your own reflections in the mirrored columns. And so, it became a relatively concise account, as they were not alone, and anyone could have long ears, and you never knew who.

Anna received an update, which also included that the preliminary tally of jewellery amounted to 210 valuable rings, including 150 with diamonds, 102 brooches, 50 of these with diamonds, 88 necklaces and chains with medallions, 10 ladies' chains, 10 sets of cufflinks and collar studs, 12 pairs of diamond-set cufflinks, 5 pairs of earrings, 15 bracelets, 15 tie pins, and several other items with gemstones, such as cigarette cases with diamonds. Total value 48,756 kr. It was sufficient for a new article but nowhere near enough to satisfy Anna's curiosity – nor Christian's desire not only to explain but perhaps also to discuss the case and – if lucky – get some ideas for the investigation.

A cafe was not a viable solution, but right now there were no other options, unless they could meet at the newsroom. They probably couldn't, since Anna hadn't suggested it. She wasn't alone at her workplace, where the interest would likely be just as intense and might tempt Bærentzen to interfere and make insinuating remarks.

In the paper, Anna had to share the space with 'The Demise of Advertisement Agent Edvard Mønsted'. He had been drinking heavily with a Mr Hansen and had then needed to relieve himself. A trip to the yard had led to tripping on the cobblestones, after which he had been carried into the back room of a tailor's shop to sleep it off. He had got up again sometime in the night, never to return from another trip to the yard. It wasn't a case for the police; the death was considered natural.

Anna's own story from the big world was much more dramatic – a murder on the train to Paris. A Madame Guerin had been attacked by two soldiers, one of whom strangled her while the other smashed her head in, after which they threw the body onto the tracks. The loot: 5 francs. The scandal was complete when word got out that one of the robbers was the son of a police inspector. The whole of Paris – indeed, the whole of France – were outraged. There was even an illustration sent from Paris. Bærentzen certainly couldn't complain that she was too delicate or ignored other foreign stories.

3.

Constable Jacobsen arrived at the main post office and found a suitable spot by the forms where he could keep an eye on the counter for poste restante without being conspicuous. He stood pen in hand and a form on the desk, looking pensive – eyes on the room – as if he were trying to remember an address. After a couple of hours, a gentleman appeared at the counter, asking for letters for S. Butzehau, which prompted a very discreet signal to Jacobsen, who quickly learned that it was the same person who had also collected mail for Kemprer. Jacobsen hurried after the man, and apprehended him.

Christian went to the local police station to inspect the detainee, who was told to empty his pockets under the supervision of Christian and Jacobsen. Their contents turned out to be a wallet with various letters addressed to Vaclav Brezina, Møntergade 14, 4, care of Mrs Olsen, a business card with the name J. Golombek Jr., Copenhagen, a nut, a purse with 2 kroner, 62 øre, and two foreign copper coins, three keys, a toiletry case, a fob watch, and a pocket knife. Everything duly recorded.

It was harder going extracting any information from the man himself for the simple reason that he barely spoke Danish and neither German nor Russian, only Polish and Bohemian. Name: Vaclav Brezina, born August 23, 1881, in Velin in Bohemia. Confectioner's assistant at Haugsted, Kjøbenhavn's Dragee-Bonbons Factory, in Nyhavn. So far, primarily thanks to the business card and the envelopes. It didn't bode well, as the men at the cafe had spoken German, but his lack of language proficiency could, of course, be due to the fact that he was talking to the police.

Later in the day, he was presented to Einar Madsen from Automat Caféen, who didn't recognise him. He wasn't one of the German brothers with the abundance of mail, so who was he? Totally innocent or? Regardless, it would be necessary to find out more from both the landlady and the bonbon factory. At the Detective Office, Madsen sat with Christian and detective inspector Schou. Christian summarised:

- He says his name is Vaclav Brezina, and he's born in Bohemia. He speaks poor Danish, works at the bonbon factory in Nyhavn 31, lives in Møntergade with Mrs Olsen, and knows absolutely nothing about anyone named Kemprer. He often collects letters, but they're for himself or a J. Golombek or Butzgehau, which is a name Golombek uses, and it's made up because the letters are from his Danish girlfriend, whose father mustn't know. And he's never set foot in Automat Caféen. He has given us permission to search his lodgings. He says he's completely innocent and isn't in possession of stolen goods, and he's legally registered as a resident alien at Station 2. He has been presented to dishwasher Einar Madsen from Automat Caféen, who says he's not one of the two suspicious ones.

Madsen rubbed his forehead.

- Find Golombek – and Kemprer, if he even exists –
and talk to Mrs Olsen and the factory manager.

Before Christian left, a letter arrived from Aalborg from
an enthusiastic contractor named Olsen, who had
evidently read the newspapers – they were all filled with
stories about 'The Great Jewel Robbery', and the usual
lot – as well as new ones like Mr Olsen – were eager to
contribute to the investigation. In this case, with
information from the Norwegian capital, Kristiania,
where the contractor had been on a business trip and
met a lady in the street. She spoke Danish, so they went
to a restaurant and had a couple of drinks. Then she
became chatty and explained that she and her husband
made a living selling watches and jewellery – or
pawning them – in Stockholm, Trondheim, and St.
Petersburg. Items purchased in Copenhagen and
Germany, but she couldn't quite remember where. The
couple had plans to buy a shop on Vesterbrogade in
Copenhagen and deal in raffle tickets. The contractor
had asked about the goods but didn't have any money
ready, so could they meet again the next day? She
disappeared. She had explained that her husband was
29, Danish, named Christian Jensen, and if the
contractor would be so kind as to pretend not to
recognise her and not to greet her were they to meet
randomly in the street and she was in the company of
someone else? The lady was described as around 22,
pale, red-haired, of medium height, and wearing a black

raincoat. Christian read the letter again. According to the contractor, he had met her a couple of months ago. She had apparently made an indelible impression, and under the circumstances, one could suspect that the aforementioned jewellery, obtained in Copenhagen and Germany, could stem from burglaries, given that time and money were spent on disposing of them in other countries. The contractor's suspicion was well-founded. Schou was handed the letter and telegraphed his colleagues in Kristiania, Trondheim, Stockholm, Hamburg, and Berlin to inquire if they knew anything about the couple. They did not.

Christian went to Brezina's lodgings, where Mrs Olsen let him in. It was a completely ordinary room, inhabited by a completely ordinary bachelor. A bed, a table, a chair, a wardrobe, a washstand, a dresser... There was nothing immediately evident that could be related to either jewel thefts or any other criminal activity. There weren't many things besides the necessities, like a razor, extra braces, Sunday clothes, and soap, and nothing that in any way indicated that the resident had money to spend. Christian found a bank book, where savings were accumulated from wages, a bundle of letters matching those found in his pocket, and a mysterious embroidered piece, perhaps from a girlfriend left behind in Bohemia? It lay alongside his passport, some letters from Bohemia and what was probably a birth certificate folded around the registration paper for foreigners, in a cigar box in the top drawer of the dresser. The visit to the bonbon factory provided even less reason to believe that he could be involved in anything. Praise from the boss as friendly, sociable, and punctual – if only everyone were like him. Brezina could quite safely be taken off the list of suspects.

The list of stolen goods was finally complete and added to the police gazette, filling several pages. Jewellery worth more than 48,000 kr. – a staggering amount. A large poster was also made describing the jewellery and displayed in several places in the city, in case anyone found them or encountered anyone trying to sell them.

A visit to Helena brought no news – nothing was for sale, and no one had tried to pay with jewellery to anyone she knew. The market seemed almost closed – perhaps because right now it would be quite impossible to get rid of so much as a cufflink without arousing suspicion. But it was also Helena's turn to ask.

- So?
- So, what?
- Seen her again?
- Yes, actually I have.

Christian chuckled.

- You were right, which is quite miraculous. But it's strictly professional.

And I'm the Queen of Sheba.

- You *are* the Queen of Sheba.

Christian patted the purple velvet cushions he sat on and looked around her boudoir, which was beginning to resemble the decor of a sultan's harem.

- It's getting more splendid every day.
- I'm not complaining.

The next morning, Anna and Christian met again at La Glace; this time by prior arrangement, to avoid any more 'incidents' at the Detective Office, but the morning customers at a cafe are mostly regulars, so it wasn't a viable permanent solution, unless they wanted to become an 'incident' at the cafe – or worse still – in a rival newspaper. They felt exposed, mostly because they behaved differently, and it was impossible not to notice when they tried to make space for both cups and papers.

The political situation in Europe could lead people to believe they were dealing in information and were spies. There were plenty of those everywhere, and if they looked in the mirrors, it could seem like everyone was watching them. Christian could not risk being reported for espionage, which could prompt a lot of unwanted questions from Madsen, who might not find it just as insanely amusing as Bærentzen undoubtedly would if Anna were reported as a spy.

The unease led to a quick decision that cafes and cafe tables were not suitable for meetings, so Anna did the absolutely unthinkable but unquestionably practical thing and invited Christian to her home, even though they weren't even on familiar terms.

Home turned out to be a large room with its own entrance in Anna's parents' vast apartment in Kronprinsessegade. The flat was originally designed with the idea that a family would have a son who would eventually need a bit of privacy, and until this happy moment, the room could easily have a lodger without inconvenience to the family. Hence the separate entrance via the back staircase and, of course, also with a door leading into the apartment, so the lodger – or son – could join at meals, and the maid had easy access for cleaning.

Anna's mother had ensured that standards were upgraded at the same time as the rest of the apartment when provided with electricity and new bathrooms, so there was now electric light throughout the flat, a gas water heater in the kitchen and bathrooms – one in Anna's, where there was also a WC. They also got a telephone.

Anna had no siblings, so she had been given the room by her liberal mother, who had also equipped it with conveniences like a queen size bed, a large wardrobe, a huge desk, a folding table with two chairs, two padded armchairs, large bookcases, and some modern paintings. Christian was impressed.

Anna fetched refreshments from the kitchen herself, relieved that Marie apparently was out shopping, and decided that given the circumstances, they might as well be on first-name terms. Christian agreed. They sat down at the table with tea, bread, butter, and cheese.

- Worried about break-ins?

Christian pointed at the foils on the wall.

- Not particularly. I have a Schouboe under the pillow.

- You what?

- Relax. I'm kidding. It's in a drawer.

- You have a gun?

- Yes indeed. And a permit.

- And you hit the target every time, I presume?

Anna laughed and thought, 'let's see what he's made of.' She rummaged in a drawer and found a stack of shooting targets, where one could put a stick through the one hole in the middle, and handed them to Christian, who whistled.

- Have you considered a career in the police?

- Nah. Bank robber. Better money.

- Absolutely. Can you handle other instruments besides ones that make holes in people?

- I'm pretty good at the piano.

It turned out there was plenty of space on the desk for all sorts of papers, and there were very comfortable furnishings for drinking tea as well, where, in addition to discussing possible criminal scenarios, they also easily delved into the global situation. It suddenly became important to keep an eye on the time via the clock on the wall, which was a family heirloom. The arms were moving way too fast.

*
**

Christian spent the afternoon tracking down Samuel Kemprer, born in Lotz, supposedly living at Øresundsgade 30, 1, rear house, sharing a room with another man. He accompanied Schou to the address, where no one was at home. Instead, they found the house owner – a carpenter's apprentice named Jensen, who had no idea where the lodgers were or where they might have moved on to. But if the gentlemen detectives could just wait a moment. Jensen went inside and rummaged through a chest of drawers and came back with a photo:

- This is Kemprer.
- May we borrow the picture?
- Of course.

They went on a long walk around the city, where neither the dishwasher at Automat Caféen nor Brezina, who was still in custody, recognised Kemprer from the photograph. They continued to Turesensgade 7, where Russian interpreter Christian Golombe lived. He knew Golombek well:

- He's my brother, Jacob Golombek – he lives at Lille Kongensgade 20, 3rd floor.

Christian showed Golombe the photo.

- That's Samuel Kemprer. What about him?

Nothing, it turned out, and there was no explanation as to why the two brothers couldn't agree on how to spell their surname. They also stopped by clerk L. C. Andersen at Mende's, who had seen the mysterious men in Kronprinsensgade, but no, it wasn't one of them in the picture. The postal clerk was also shown the photograph and confirmed that Golombek had collected letters along with Brezina, but they had nothing to do with Kemprer. He must have got it wrong.

The next day, the rumour had apparently reached Kemprer himself, so he showed up at the Detective Office on his own accord and explained that he received money from his father in Lotz every week, and from his brother who lived in Hamburg. He was smart enough to bring some letters as proof and was then handed back the ones they had confiscated at the post office. There was – just as he had explained – a 5-Reichsmark note in the envelope from his father. Christian wrote a report explaining that no one was home, no one's residence had anything resembling stolen goods, and people were who they said they were, and so Brezina was released and the fingerprint sheets sent to the archive.

Christian, Schou, and Madsen looked resignedly at each other over Madsen's desk. A lot of work and zero progress, other than being able to shorten the list of suspects. No one had seen more of the two men from Automat Caféen, and every new inquiry had led to lots of work and a total absence of results other than folders overflowing with fingerprints at the Central Bureau of Identification. The disappointment was palpable. At least management couldn't accuse them of doing nothing. It was very poor consolation.

For Anna, today's meeting with Christian meant a whole new enthusiasm – journalist and detective – clearly an improvement and something to pursue further. She decided it was time to get more focused with the Schouboe – a gift from her mother. She looked at the clock. If she was lucky, there would still be plenty of space at the shooting range for at least another hour. That meant changing her handbag, as she only had one reinforced to handle the weight of a pistol without tearing the lining. Fashions in handbags were hopeless for working women. Even a notepad could cause problems. At least a muff would suffice in winter. It was amazing what could fit in one of those. Anna changed her mind and chose a muff. Anna appreciated pistol shooting, which required an entirely different approach from fencing. Calm, aim, visualise the trajectory of the bullet, shoot. Bullseye. Every time. Pure contemplation. 'Can you visualise the projectile's trajectory, even if you hold the pistol differently?' .... Yes. Interesting. Maybe even useful. Anna decided to practise longer than planned and not just with an outstretched arm. Images from wild west movies came to mind – there were a lot of shooting techniques to try out. At least all those without a horse. This meant that she later had to rush in to dinner, where she was met by insinuating smiles and 'we hear you had a gentleman caller', to which she replied,

- Yes – work. There's no room for case files on a cafe table, and I don't want Rasmussen poking his nose into anything at the newsroom. He's unbearable enough as it is. I'm too good at avoiding making his coffee, which is the only thing women are capable of in his mind.

The jewel thefts were then duly discussed, giving mother Agnes reinforced hopes. There was clearly a prospect of more meetings, even though it was also clear that it was the detective work and not the detective that kept Anna so fascinated. Marie must have come back before Christian left, without her hearing it, Anna noted. But she was used to jabs. Next time, she might as well let Marie bring the tea. Then she could see for herself that there was nothing going on when she lagged to the missus. And what was that book Christian had talked about? Something that ended in 'os'. Gross. There it was. And something about investigation. 'I wonder if it can be found in a local bookshop?' It certainly sounded like an interesting bedtime reading for a detective in training. She decided on a trip to Copenhagen's bookshops. If in vain, she would get it by mail order.

The evening was spent at the University of Copenhagen in the company of her mother and father, who greeted lecturer Harald Bohr, the evening's speaker, and his brother Niels Bohr, whom Anna's father William thought would certainly amount to something really big and not just on the soccer field like Harald, who played for the national team.

Christian went home, stripped off his clothes, and, as always, began his ballet exercises – plus those he had invented himself, which had earned him respect in a nightlife where you know someone who knows someone who has a mate who... and where a large part of any communication was done in body language, occasionally resulting in lasting injuries. With elegance and precision, he kicked his hat down from the top of the coat rack.

However, what had caught everyone else's attention that day was something entirely different. Engineers Berg and Storm had built a brand-new and entirely Danish aeroplane at Burmeister & Wain. Expectations were sky high for this wonder, which was 'built based on all the excellent experiences that have already been gathered in the field of aviation', so the machine would naturally prove to be 'an excellent flyer'. A 290 kg monoplane with flexible wings and rudder, meaning it was both stable and manoeuvrable. 'The machine will be tested from Amager, and the engineers plan to form a joint-stock company.' The proud engineers were photographed in front of their aeroplane, which 'everyone was looking forward to seeing in the air.' They had good reason to be proud. The machine was truly something special. Anna read Rasmussen's article as well as several others, which were very similar, and decided that she too would go to Amager when the machine was to be tested, and that aviation was something that needed closer inspection. She recalled a Da Vinci quote: 'Once you have tasted flight, you will forever walk the earth with your eyes turned skyward, for there you have been, and there you will always long to return.' It sounded likely – and very, very tempting. Anna was determined to put the quote to the test, if it was in any way possible. Poor Leonardo never had the chance.

4.

The next morning, both Anna and Christian received a telegram almost simultaneously, and both initially thought it was a mistake. It wasn't. Christian was the first to realise this as the sender of his telegram was the Royal Prussian Chief of Police in Berlin, informing him that there had been a burglary at jeweller Henry Nevir & Sohn on Potsdamer Straße 22 sometime between Saturday evening and Monday morning – most likely Sunday night. Above the jewellery store was an empty office space visible from the street. Then followed a description that greatly resembled the file on Kronprinsensgade. However, a false key had been used for the door. Boxes and various items were stacked in front of the windows on the first floor, so no one had seen any suspicious light. It too was an old building; the floor separation was as poor as at Møinichen's, and clay and plaster had been collected in – yes, an umbrella. The ladder was missing, as the hole was right above the counter, so it hadn't been necessary. The robbers had also been more meticulous – they had covered the hole in the floor upstairs with a desk carpet. The shop staff declared that there had been no unfamiliar customers in the days before – it wasn't a high street shop, so their customers were mostly regulars. There were as few traces of the perpetrators as in Copenhagen.

Christian read on about a suspect: Vilhelm Olsen, most recently sentenced to four years of hard labour and known as a very daring thief. He had been in Berlin for 5-6 days before the burglary, together with a local cabaret singer, as reported by their neighbours, while he himself had been the manager of a small hotel. Now the couple had vanished into thin air. Even his mother didn't know where he was.

The telegram from Berlin marked the beginning of another round of international correspondence. Stockholm replied they knew nothing about an Olsen or any others matching the description or fingerprints provided, but if anyone had heard of a Hasselfeldt, they would like to be informed. She was a suspect in Sweden in connection with a burglary almost identical just a few months prior. She might fit the bill, and they had photos and fingerprints from previous criminal activity. Likely in a gang and married to a known criminal. Photographs and fingerprints on the way. Christian continued his workday with Anna's last remark in his ears.

- There's something déjà vu about this. Older than Kronprinsensgade. And here in Copenhagen.

He went to the archives to discover that she was right. There had been a burglary at Jeweller Michelsen in Bredgade, but with different methods, and then another – admittedly not resulting in a burglary, but Berth's shop on Amagertorv had also had visitors – or rather almost, as the burglars hadn't made it through the ceiling from the room above. The floor separation had been too solid. The thieves had left behind a homemade rope ladder with knots made by an expert, and the rope was of either Danish or Swedish origin and from a factory. A familiar theme, but with variations.

A local petty criminal, Osvald Mortensen – also known as Osvaldo – had a couple of months ago and while incarcerated voluntarily informed that it was done by international thieves, including a Swede – Carl Johansson from Stockholm – and a German, who had come to the city to commit robberies. He had heard them plan everything, along with several other burglaries, including at least one in Stockholm. Back then, nobody had bothered listening to him, so he shut up again, was released, and disappeared. Now one could regret not listening if there had been any time for regrets.

A new detail caught the eye. The timing. Thieves working on weekends in all three cities. Christian decided to have a nice little chat with Osvaldo. Thief, con artist, petty criminal à la carte, and an old acquaintance by now, and, oddly enough, usually trustworthy. A closer check of Osvaldo's merits revealed he had been in Stockholm for a while – he had been arrested for vagrancy at least twice by the Stockholm police. It was uncertain whether he had returned home, but it was worth investigating.

Christian continued reading the old reports, which also revealed that one Axel Bernhard Nyström from Stockholm and an unknown accomplice had stayed at Hotel Cosmopolite in Store Kongensgade at the time of the attempted robbery at Berth's. Stockholm's detective force, who had of course been notified immediately, knew nothing about any Nyström – or a Karl Johansson – but they found Nyström and arrested him with a subsequent search of his home but to no avail. So, nothing else to do but release him. Karl Johansson had not been found. Perhaps Osvaldo might have heard something while in Stockholm?

Anna sat with her shorter telegram and decided likewise that it was probably time to check if there had been more burglaries like these in the past year. That meant new telegrams to the European capitals and a few more cities. Although expensive, she was sure Bærentzen wouldn't find it unnecessary. Especially if she became the first to link the robberies. Paris, Nice, London, Berlin, Vienna...

It was quite incomprehensible and very frustrating that no jewels had yet turned up for sale. However, a call from Assistenshuset – a pauper's house which also served as a pawnshop – gave the detectives new hope in that regard. A young man had come to pawn a diamond ring and was immediately detained. He explained his name was Lind and that the ring belonged to his sister, who had asked him to pawn it because she needed the money and was too shy to go herself. He was just the helpful brother. That explanation didn't hold up past the counter at Station 1, where he suffered an involuntary name-change to Aage Lars Larsen, who – would you believe – lived in Kronprinsensgade, but...

When Mr Larsen found out that the police knew who he was, he gave up the fibbing and explained that he had 'borrowed' the ring from his father, who had a jewellery store at Østergade 35, which he managed. He had also 'borrowed' other items there, which he had also pawned. He couldn't quite remember what. All to cover up his lack of bookkeeping skills, admitted the now guilt-ridden young man. A visit to his father's shop and a brief conversation with the father confirmed the ring to be worth 250 kr. and it did indeed come from his shop.

The father explained he knew nothing of his son's 'borrowing' and kindly asked the police not to pursue the matter further, as it would otherwise end up in the records – avidly read by the press and therefore a much greater risk to their future earnings than his son's pilfering. Such a stain on the business could close it. The police chose to show leniency, as it could be written off as an internal family matter unrelated to anything else. Unfortunately. The father got his ring and his son back, and Bugge archived photos and fingerprints in case the son should pick up on his inclinations at a later date. He probably wouldn't get better at bookkeeping just by getting caught, but one could hope his father would now help him with the accounts.

At the Detective Office, the pile of names, photos, descriptions, and fingerprints continued to grow along with the frustration.

5.

A new letter from Stockholm added to the pile and ended up getting the normally very calm Madsen worked up. They were getting nowhere, and it would only be couple of days before the press would start getting ironic. The latest statement from the police – a circulation of a picture and description of the sock foot – hadn't exactly improved matters, but since everything else had failed, they had to send out something that might help in any way possible. Perhaps someone had seen it before?

The newspaper still lay on the desk:

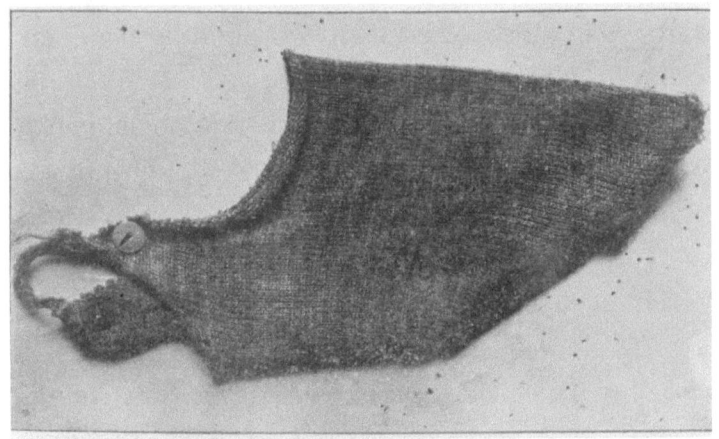

Whose is the Sock Foot?

... The Copenhagen Police have issued an illustrated description... As one will see from this elaborate piece of writing, it is pure and simple

falsehood when certain papers claim there are no Sherlock Holmeses within the Copenhagen Police. Conan Doyle couldn't have given a more conscientious literary portrayal of something as prosaic as an old sweaty sock foot. Now all that's left is to find the connection between this piece of naturalism and the jewellery theft in Kronprinsensgade.

'Ho, ho, how witty.' But it was time for a new how-far-have-we-(not)-come meeting with la Cour and Bugge, where Christian contributed to the party with the story of Osvaldo and Johansson, which for the first time got Madsen to swear. Extensively.

- Who the hell is Johansson?

Christian explained about the nearly identical burglary in Stockholm a couple of months earlier and looked as if that wasn't the whole story.

- Out with it, la Cour. It can't get any worse.

But it could, as it turned out, with the most absurd account Madsen had ever heard. Christian leafed through a letter from the Detective Office in Stockholm, which, even though written on ultra-thin paper, was thick as a book.

- The police in Stockholm have also investigated a burglary at jeweller Möllenborg from 1905 – or rather – an attempted burglary. The door to Immanuel Ries' travel agency on Drottninggatan, which was right above Möllenborg's jewellery store, was forced open with a crowbar, the desk drawer was broken into and the contents were scattered around, but there was nothing of value, so nothing was stolen. They didn't get through the floor. Two beams had been removed in three-meter lengths, but the last one was only partially cut through. The filling lay on the floor, but they hadn't broken through. Perhaps they were interrupted. Suspicion fell on three foreigners who had visited the jewellery shop together to have a fob made – and they had also been upstairs at the travel agency, where they had left a cape, providing an opportunity to come back: Romeo and Julio – no, I'm not joking – brothers, previously known for theft. Romeo is a musician. Both arrested together with an Egisto, and all denied any involvement.

Christian continued flipping through the pages and soldiered on:

- Julio came to Stockholm in the company of an unknown man and was arrested but had to be released due to lack of evidence. Romeo had sent a suitcase to Brussels, which the police had seized on arrival, and which turned out to contain tools that could be used for such a burglary. The suitcase was sent from Marseille – and yes, there had also been a burglary there similar to the others. Perhaps they were all from Marseille. Down there, Romeo went by the name Astena, and he lived there with an Edouard Morelli – presumed member of the same gang, which Stockholm now referred to as the 'the wall breakers'. The Marseille gang also include a police officer without fixed abode – Julio Cesare Augusto Beniamina, 31, who was extradited to Sweden, where he couldn't be convicted due to lack of evidence.

He was later arrested again in Marseille together with a Pierre Polombi, 29, without fixed abode and sentenced to two years in prison for burglary. The gang leader is Augusto Darvia, 48. He calls himself a jeweller and lived with his wife Aiola in Marseille until the end of September last year, when they both disappeared without a trace. He had already been arrested several times – four times for pick-pocketing, but released due to lack of evidence. Apparently, a cosmopolitan gentleman just like Beniamini. Darvia's photo has been shown to some people who might have seen him with unknown persons, including a 'professor', but Julio claimed not to know him. The gentlemen were also seen in Paris – Julio, Darvia, an Arbarelli, and perhaps one more called Martin Saumenbluhm living in Rue de la Paix no. 10, also claiming to be a jeweller and a dealer in pearls, and whom the police suspects of fencing as well. He was arrested in Nice in connection with a jewellery theft – through the ceiling. And released due to – you've guessed it – lack of evidence.

Christian remembered Anna's remarks about a burglary in Nice. There was much to discuss next time. He continued, undeterred.

- The police in Nice informs that Julio's gang also includes Edouard Marelli, Jean Cyclone, Louis Buccitti, Henri Crezenzi, Maria Marras, Alfred Merlani, Louise Mannueli, and Antonio Peseauti. The police have confiscated various correspondence – mostly from Julio to Romeo, where it is clear that during a stay in

Freuering, Julio committed crimes, mainly described in euphemistic terms.

Christian rifled through several more pages with pictures, descriptions, and multiple sets of fingerprints.

- It sounds like the cast of an opera. Peseuati, alias Alexandre alias Count of Pierini alias Count Pierrici alias Cerri Nicolai. And a José Alvarado, who was arrested in Marseille for breaking into a jewellery shop – through the ceiling, of course – and Giovanni Bruzzoni and Carlo Christe... They've sent a *very* long list from Stockholm. It must have taken ages to compile.

Beniamini Julio Cesare Augusto,
alias Ostega Fernandez.

Madsen buried his face in his hands and groaned. The next news articles wouldn't just be ironic. They'd be sarcastic. For starters. Not to mention the variety shows. Romeo and Julio with a full opera cast. 'Say it isn't true.' He could almost hear the refrains already. And see the chorus girls. And hear the trumpets blaring. It was Bugge who summed it up:

- So, there's been almost an epidemic of burglaries of the same kind. The Swedes are holding on to Romeo and Julio, and the Germans suspect an Olsen. So, what do we think? The same ones or copycats? No one has found the same fingerprints in two places so far, and none of the jewels have turned up – neither ours nor theirs. I've sent what we've got to Stockholm – they've sent us what la Cour is reading from. At least our local Russians are out of the picture.

Christian thought of the next meeting with Anna with anticipation – but first, he had to make a trip to the post office, where, as expected, there was a cream-coloured envelope with a coat of arms addressed to Chretien, Conte de Namours, BP 213, Copenhague. Time to stretch his legs again. A more than welcome interruption in an apparently fruitless investigation with only one bright spot – Anna.

Christian visited Anna and expressed his desperation – and Madsen's – as well as their expectations of extensive journalistic sarcasm. Unfortunately, Anna also reacted like a journalist at first. Romeo and Julio? Some headlines write themselves, and this was one of them, and the police would just have to live with it, no matter how reluctantly. In Christian's case, compensated by tea and cake and endless patience for long explanations with food in his mouth. As Madsen had also said – there were now enough suspects to populate a provincial town. And surrounding villages. Anna thought of the boarding school in Switzerland – had she met girls with those names? Not that she could remember. It was completely different things that had stuck in her memory. A certain expertise with locks, for example. Anna smiled inwardly at the thought that the most effective jail breakers and burglars she knew were teenage girls at boarding schools. But she didn't recognise the names. Instead, she explained to Christian that she had sent telegrams to the major newspapers in the European capitals and a couple more about any similar type of burglaries, and promised he would get a list as soon as she had written an article.

- So, we have a Swedish thief, an Italian gang, some mysterious individuals, said to resemble Germans, but others think look like English footballers, a Russian Jew, a Pole, a French fence, an old burglary in Nice, one in Marseille, two in Stockholm, and a new burglary in Berlin. Oh yes – and one newspaper calls it American methods...

- So, all you need now is a couple of Chinese or maybe a Mexican. Don't you worry. They'll show up tomorrow. Wearing sock feet.

Christian sent her a murderous look.

- Easy now. Everyone is impressed with the fantastic description. Several newspapers even write that 'some papers' – note the quotation marks – must be mistaken when they think you're short of a Sherlock Holmes. Even Conan Doyle should be impressed. Detective Holmes?

- Elementary, my dear Miss Lendorph. Good Lord. But yes, the description is thorough. That's sort of the point. And it's Bugge's description – not mine.

They agreed that an address on Rue de la Paix would be the ideal location for a fence and something worth investigating.

- Unfortunately, it's the business of the gendarmerie in Paris and therefore not something we can handle from Copenhagen. We will, of course, write and ask, but it could take some time to get the inquiry through the French bureaucracy.

6.

There were now so many suspects in so many places that it was decided Bugge should go on a tour with photos and fingerprints – including to Stockholm and Kristiania, so Christian was left alone on the case for a few days, awaiting Bugge's return, unless something happened.

Mrs Vonsild called, and Christian took another trip to Købmagergade. Last Saturday, Mrs Vonsild explained to Christian, who was now sitting at a workbench in the back room with a good cup of coffee and unlimited patience, she had been about to close the shop, so everything was dark, and all that was left to do was to lock the back door. Then two men showed up in the street. A medium height, light-haired, beardless, slim man about 20 years old and a slightly darker, taller man with a thin moustache. She hadn't noticed their clothes. They didn't look like regular customers for a jeweller's shop – at least not through the front door – and they were very busy looking at the windows. They couldn't see her; she was invisible in the darkness of the shop, so they took their time, and she didn't dare move. Eventually, they left. Since then, she had kept an eye out, but no one resembling those two had shown up – at least not yet. Christian took notes and wrote descriptions. That meant new telegrams – Hamburg, Warnemünde, Kiel, Altona, Lübeck, Bremen, Kristiania,

Kristiansand, Stockholm, Malmö, Lund, Landskrona, Trelleborg, and Gothenburg – and phone calls to Helsingør, Aarhus, Frederikshavn, Nyborg, Gedser, Korsør, and Esbjerg in case anyone matching these descriptions tried to leave the country or showed up at a railway station.

The next day, there was a reply from the Detective Office in Lund, who hadn't seen anyone as described, but they had, however, apprehended two marines from the American battleship Louisiana. The two marines had tried to sell two gold rings to a goldsmith in town. He had read about the burglary in Copenhagen and immediately notified the police. And then the disappointment. Again. One of the marines, of Swedish descent, had bought the rings in a port town in France and was going to use the money to visit his uncle, who lived near Lund. The relationship was confirmed by both the uncle and the American navy. However, they couldn't confirm that the rings were bought in France, so perhaps they came from Møinichen? He stated he hadn't had a gold ring with five opals or one with a diamond and two sapphires, so no. Same answer from Berlin – the rings didn't come from there either. Copenhagen suggested they ask about the rings with the police in Marseille and Nice. After all, the marines would be easy to locate again, if necessary. The police in Lund handed the marines back to the Commander of the Louisiana, who promised they wouldn't go ashore anywhere until they had answers from Nice and Marseille.

Bugge wrote back from Stockholm that he hadn't had any more luck, but he confirmed that his colleague Bergmann could order more filing cabinets for the Central Bureau of Identification, and he would bring a suitcase full of photos and descriptions himself. So, at least Bergmann was happy. Bugge could also report that no one he had spoken to had heard of the red-haired young lady with a Danish husband who planned to start a lottery shop on Vesterbrogade. Visits to pawnbrokers in both Stockholm and Kristiania also yielded nothing. Apparently, only the entrepreneur from Aalborg remembered her. Christian thought the couple might well be on a 'shopping trip' in Germany.

The rest of the day offered a jumble of information from near and far. A man called to explain he had seen suspicious ladies and gentlemen on the train to Farum; said ladies probably of easy virtue. A closer examination revealed there was only one lady, and she was more lightweight than loose-living. Her name was Sylvia Bjerring, and she was a dancer at the Moorish Hall. The gentlemen were foreigners, which in itself was of course suspicious, unless, as it turned out, they were musicians at the Moorish Hall and therefore entirely generic suspects with no connection whatsoever to neither the burglaries nor any other crime. For Christian, the interrogation of the musicians had meant a very entertaining conversation in French, learning some new

Parisian phrases, he was looking forward to trying out on Anna, although they were a bit Apache.

Later in the evening, Christian went to the ball at the Countess of Chambord's and was, as usual, greeted by the hostess herself:

- Conte!

The countess was beaming as she – also, as usual – handed him the dance card along with payment for the evening's services. It only took a second to make the money disappear into a pocket and open the card, which, of course, was full – mostly with names he knew.

- Mademoiselle Antoinette?

- La jolie brune qui parle avec le colonel de la Calmette.

The countess of Chambord discreetly nodded towards a young, dark-haired girl. Christian followed her gaze and found a lovely young brunette he hadn't seen before, next to Colonel de la Calmette. He nodded again and continued reading, bowed, clicked his heels, and the countess signalled with an elegant hand gesture for the orchestra to start the waltz. Christian found the first fortunate lady and bowed. He danced all night with beautiful young – and some older – ladies, who surrendered themselves to the strong arms of this fairytale prince and floated across the floor, eyes and jewels sparkling under the chandeliers. And Christian became one with the music, dancing through the night interrupted only by champagne, bubbling in harmony with the music, already fizzing in his blood.

The next morning, an unusually slow and blurry-eyed detective la Cour, received a message from Berlin with a notice for Salvatore Barbaria, Max Katchinski and Ferdinand Mönch with wife and child, and news of a reward of 3000 marks for the recovery of the jewels and 500 for the capture of the perpetrator. It took about half an hour for the last of the champagne bubbles to burst, so the letters in the telegram began to form words and make sense. Christian tried to think, but it was tough going. He had never heard those names before.

Anna sat at the typewriter and the beginning of an article:

Romeo and Julio.

A Franco-Italian Criminal Gang at Play in Copenhagen?

when Bærentzen came in and went over to read over her shoulder with a smile that quickly turned into a grin.

- That's front page and no mistake. Pure gold. Tell me!

Anna had to explain in detail. Bærentzen was a happy editor. So happy, in fact, he invited Anna to lunch so they could talk about Conan Doyle, whom their colleagues had so kindly referred to. Anna had to provide some insider knowledge about the author, who apparently had gone a bit gaga – at least in Bærentzen's eyes – with seances and spiritualism and the like. That was true, Anna explained. He did actually travel, giving lectures on spiritualism as far away as Toronto in Canada. Bærentzen was puzzled. Hadn't anyone got any the wiser since Madame Blavatsky? His admiration cooled slightly.

At their afternoon meeting, Anna and Christian discussed the reward and the American marine, and Christian got the chance to steer the conversation towards Monsieur Lecoq as an excuse to speak French, so he could try out his new vocabulary. As expected, Anna didn't bat an eyelid. Instead, she taught him some other phrases, apparently popular at international boarding schools for girls. He was impressed. Again. Afterwards, they had a long conversation about the difference between a Pieper, the Navy's Francotti, the English Webleys, and the Danish Schouboe. Christian suggested that a Webley 320 would be easier to carry in a handbag since it weighed less, and the barrel was shorter. In fact, it was quite small. He could hide one in his hand. Anna was unusually impressed and decided to investigate the matter further as soon as Christian was out the door. He didn't tell her that his mother had one exactly because it was easier to carry in a handbag. Nor did he tell her it was Helena who had bought it for her from a client. And she had one too.

Later in the evening, Christian visited Helena, who had no news about the jewels – or Osvaldo – and didn't have time for a casual chat. On his way out, Helena adjusted his hat, stopped, sniffed his breath, and then his wrist.

- Too much champagne yesterday. Not a pleasant smell to get close to.

She winked at him. Christian chose to continue at some of the city's lesser-known taverns – often on the first and second floors of back buildings without a sign on the door but with decent beer and dishes like 'half an owl with feathers' on the menu (1.50 kr.), and where the smell of yesterday's champagne wouldn't bother anyone. He ended up at Schooner-Larsen's and had a chat with old acquaintances holding no grudge against him for arresting them regularly – especially not as he was generous with rounds and even a carafe. After all, both they and he were just doing their job. But no one had heard anything about Osvaldo returning. Nor about any unusual dealings in jewellery.

However, Schooner-Larsen had a question for him, too. Had Christian heard anything about what had become of Leaning-Inger, who hadn't been seen for a few days now? They were getting worried. He hadn't, so he decided to call on his old colleague Nielsen and ask him to stop by Inger's place to see if she had once again been beaten up so badly, she couldn't walk and needed to be taken to the hospital.

At the Detective Office, Christian discovered that there were Copenhageners who were also fond of the supernatural, as the day brought a letter from Marie Jensen on Borups Allé:

'With these lines, I would like to inquire if I have permission to independently investigate a theft. The other night, I saw in my sleep a man hiding some of the stolen jewels. I can recognise the place. Respectfully.'

Christian went to see Madsen to ask if there were standard procedures for such cases. The seriousness – or rather desperation – of the situation was evident when, instead of the usual glance from Madsen that would have meant 'there's definitely room for you in the loony bin', he received a deep sigh and a question about whether he thought she could have overheard some conversation about it and thought she had dreamed it? In Christian's experience, you could indeed hear what was happening in the courtyard, even from a fifth-floor flat, if the window was open. They jointly decided to send Jacobsen to visit Miss Jensen, although it was far-fetched in every possible way.

Contrary to expectations, the day also brought hope. The Detective Office in Stockholm sent a telegram explaining they had arrested Vilhelm Emil Ulrik Olsen and Wilhelmine Bertha Amand Hasselfelt, suspected of, among other things, the jewel theft in Berlin. Could they have something to do with Copenhagen too? Photographs and fingerprints to follow by mail. Bugge pondered whether to call himself 'postmaster general'. The correspondence was becoming enormous. Berlin confirmed it was the right Olsen. He had been sentenced to four years of hard labour in Hamburg for defrauding a widow in collaboration with the widow's maid.

The volume of international correspondence had not escaped Madsen's attention either, and he sent a thank-you note to Jørgensen. La Cour's language skills had become more necessary than anyone could ever have imagined. The case clearly showed that crime was international, so police cooperation had to be as well, and with La Cour on the case, he didn't have to wait to have things translated. Even the anonymous letters that always surfaced in connection with major cases receiving a lot of press coverage were now coming in foreign languages – this time in German:

Many gold and jewels are coming to Copenhagen from Altona with prostitutes and pimps who have lived in Mecklenburg for 3 years and since April in Copenhagen by the name Jost or Gust...'

From 'the secret Detective'.

Christian was handed the letter and the follow-up. They could at least find out if there was a Jost or Gust living in Copenhagen. There was a Gust: Karl Friedrich Martin Gust, residing at Lille Strandstræde 6, third floor, with Andersen. A popular cigar factory worker with a cook girlfriend in Vestervoldgade. Son of farmer Carl Gust and Louise Strübing. Trained as a cigar maker in his hometown, which he left for Hamburg and Altona and finally Copenhagen, where manufacturer Eliasen in Lille Strandstræde informed them, he was an exemplary employee.

Christian listened to Gust's explanations with great patience – and pauses – which prompted Gust to explain even more. It worked every time. The shady bits of Gust's past turned out to involve women – he had left a widow in Altona, with whom he had three children, and arguments with her had led him to travel to Copenhagen. And here was perhaps the reason for the letter. He had travelled with his cousin's daughter, Erna Anna Marie Gust, whom he had known since she was a little girl. His guess – and Christian's after the long talk – was that the letter was probably from Erna's father, who was a master blacksmith in Kumerow. He was very upset that his daughter had left with Gust for Copenhagen. He had written to his daughter before, calling Gust a pimp and a scoundrel.

Gust explained about arguments between Erna and her father, even while she still lived at home, and that she had moved into a boarding house in Copenhagen and thus lived entirely on her own and was a good girl. He had nothing going on with Erna; they had just travelled together from Altona because she wasn't happy about travelling alone. It sounded plausible enough, and Christian took yet more fingerprints, which also did not match any crime scene, whether in Copenhagen or abroad. Gust's behaviour towards the widow and the three children was not Christian's problem. The blacksmith's letter was filed and instantly forgotten about.

Next summary meeting once again clarified that they had made no progress despite an extensive effort spanning most of Europe and with enough fingerprint sheets to wallpaper a large estate – yet none matched anyone at a crime scene. Where was the connection? And why hadn't any jewels surfaced from any of the thefts?

Anna and Christian entertained themselves with the same questions over Anna's cluttered desk. Where was the connection? There had to be one, and the jewels must have ended up somewhere. But where? And as what? Whole, dismantled, melted down, or just packed in a suitcase on its way across the Atlantic?

- Let's take another look at those Italians. Gang leader Augusto Darvia was a jeweller and friends with a Martin Saumenbluhm in Rue de la Paix in Paris – also a jeweller and a pearl dealer – and with a perfect address. And then there's the constable and the professor and the whole opera cast up to and including Count Pierrini...

A name suddenly seemed familiar to Christian, but one he absolutely couldn't discuss with Anna – though she noticed his face momentarily change before he declared,

- It must be the jewellers. Maybe they're altering the jewels?

- Is that something we can find out?

- It will be difficult. The word 'bureaucracy' isn't French for nothing, so it could take a while. They're happy to cooperate, but...

The conclusion was that there wasn't really anything more to write about in the newspaper right now, as a string of names, which the police themselves had difficulty keeping track of, would pose even bigger problems for the readers, who had so far only heard of Romeo and Julio. Anna had to solemnly swear not to mention Marie's letter in the columns, as it would be unfair to Marie. Anna agreed. There was no reason to expose her just because there wasn't any more interesting news, so she simply didn't include it in the report to Bærentzen. Hopefully, there would soon be replies from the European newspapers about similar thefts in their respective capitals.

Anna remembered a former schoolmate from Lausanne, whose family lived in Paris. If she was back home, she might visit a certain jeweller in Rue de la Paix in search of jewels that would match a specific dress? For example, some resembling those from Møinichen's shop. She decided to write to Jeanne. She had the number of the police gazette with the description of the jewels on her desk at the newsroom. When she checked the list, she wasn't happy. Most of the jewels were quite ordinary – except for one necklace and a charivari, both with a spider in a web. Custom work perhaps? In any case, they would be recognisable, but also so unique that it could be difficult to come up with an excuse to look for exactly that. Maybe she should just inquire about a ring with a large emerald surrounded by diamonds? After all, there was presumably a limited supply of such items, and there might be a stamp – C.J.M. It was certainly worth a try. If Saumenbluhm had the spider jewels, perhaps they were on display because of their rarity.

After another visit from her son, Ida la Cour decided things were progressing satisfactorily without her intervention. She therefore – along with her equally interested husband – contented herself with listening to the story of Romeo and Julio and the cryptic letter, the brief allusions to the meetings with Anna, and, most importantly, that it seemed the new colleagues had become nicer, and there was probably no longer any cause for concern on that front. Ida was relieved. Christian was happier than he had been in a long time, despite the hassle of solving the case. And Anna sounded like just the right one for her son. One was allowed hope.

Christian gradually learned that life at the Detective Office differed vastly from life at Nørrebro Police Station. There, it had been a small world comprising familiar characters – colleagues, drunks, prostitutes, thieves, pickpockets, businessmen and con artists. All local and some you eventually got to know, either because you found their stolen items or arrested them carrying someone else's. Occasionally, someone came along from outside, but only sporadically and mostly one at a time. A manageable world, where you found your place in the hierarchy and achieved respect or lack thereof based on merit. At the Detective Office, it was almost the opposite. Every case was from scratch. New people, new places, new everything. Maybe it did resemble being a journalist? Christian thought fondly of Anna, who had to deliver something new every day – from Peking or Paris, Nice or New York – it mattered not as long as it was entertaining. He did not choose his own cases; they came tumbling unto his desk as a result of others' actions. Just as unpredictable, almost as scattered in geography, with names and descriptions and photos in one big mess. It was like learning a new ballet from scratch – new score, new choreography – and with an entirely new ensemble – each time there was a fresh case. Or like this one – one case that kept delivering an absurd chaos of suspects.

Christian was glad that his brain was trained to remember vast amounts of information – now with an extra layer of legal knowledge from books that had not really made sense before he became a police officer. Suddenly, all the terms had faces, and crimes became people and actions that were no longer theoretical with 'if this then that'. They often turned out to have an internal logic when explained. He could not think of anyone he had arrested who hadn't believed their actions had been unavoidable and entirely justified. Sometimes he had to agree with the delinquent – sometimes the logic was as spiritual as it could only get after a bottle of brandy, often rather more.

Although his own life had started at Nørrebro, the experiences from his upbringing had been down-to-earth and colourful, and then he had moved on to the theatre's equally colourful but decidedly unearthly world. Nevertheless, it had been a surprise after all the legal intricacies to see what it was really all about. People and what they did to other people. He could still be surprised at what they could come up with. The repertoire at the Detective Office was broader than at Nørrebro or any theatre stage. And far more brutal.

Nielsen reported back on Leaning-Inger, that no one answered at the address, and no one had seen her for almost a week now. Neither she nor the drunken sailor of a boyfriend was there, and the place felt abandoned. There was no food in the bag on a string by the window, and the only piece of bread he could find was so dry a rat would break its teeth on it. It didn't sound good. Christian had written a message delivered to Helena, asking her to ask around. It wasn't like Inger to totally disappear like that. Usually, her thirst would ensure she turned up somewhere – either to steal or to beg and then find the nearest pub. But she was gone and not reported missing. But of course, who would have bothered?

7.

When Christian received his next dance invitation, he decided to be a bit more attentive and drink a little less champagne, but the evening remained short of Italian counts, and Christian soothed his disappointment with bubbles as he floated across the floor with lady after lady after lady... just one dance with each of them, otherwise there wouldn't be enough Christian to go around. The countess of Chambord also made sure she got a spot on his dance card, so she too got to have just one dance with a partner who could dance her to the stars and back again. He was truly divine, she noted contentedly.

When the ball was over, Christian walked as usual down the street and into a doorway, where he removed the Russian order, he had around his neck and the elegant moustache that only belonged in the ballroom. Both went into his inner pocket. Perhaps he should take a detour and clear his head, which was still bubbling? He couldn't do anything about the smell of champagne on his skin, which Helena had kindly referred to, except increase the dose of Penhaligon's Hammam Bouquet, which would be even more conspicuous.

As Christian almost danced down Silkegade, he heard a sound. In a room above jeweller Rungwald at Købmagergade 9, three people were engaged in the exact same exercise as in Kronprinsensgade. They had carefully stacked boxes in front of the windows on the first floor and were drilling holes in the floor so they could gain access to the jewellery shop below. They had laid their tool bag on the table beside them and were completely focused on the drilling, when one of them, who had to move sideways to continue drilling, accidentally hit the table leg with his foot. The bag of tools fell to the floor with a crash loud enough to be heard in the quiet street.

Christian stopped and instinctively looked towards the sound, which seemed to come from above almost right in front of him in Købmagergade. It didn't take a second to realise that it came from a room with something stacked in front of the windows with barely visible light – just above a jeweller's shop. The bubbles in Christian's head immediately burst, and he leaped into the stairwell and up the stairs, while others leaped down. The first one on the way down hit him in the chest, causing him to fall onto the landing, and he didn't get to see the face of neither him nor the one following, who was so fast that Christian didn't have time to react before he was gone. But the third... He had apparently hesitated, because when he came running at full speed, Christian was almost back on his feet, and he took up the pursuit, which became long and arduous.

Whoever the man was, he was agile and fast and accustomed to navigating through the Copenhagen alleys and backyards, where carts and dustbins only meant leverage, not obstacles. What the fleeing man hadn't anticipated was that the man in the evening suit pursuing him could keep up and eventually catch him, when his foot got stuck in a dustbin lid collapsing under his weight. Christian overpowered the still unknown person and calmly tied his hands with his bowtie. Neither of them had tried that before. It was also new to Pedersen, who was on the night shift, and locked up the unknown man until they could deal with him in the morning.

Christian looked more than battered – his shirt was no longer white, and his trousers were torn.

- Always a feast to arrest a burglar?

Pedersen attempted and received a weary look as he locked up the delinquent.

- See you in the morning.

A quick pat on his inner pocket reassured Christian that he hadn't lost anything, so he went straight home and fell instantly asleep. The consequences of the hunt came with the morning light, when the effects of a plentiful supply of bruises and scrapes broke through the last remnants of champagne. At least he was fit enough that his muscles didn't join in the protest.

The reception at the Detective Office was enthusiastic. Unfortunately, it included a lot of back patting, which made Christian startle as everyone without exception hit the same bruise – including Madsen, who beamed like a little sun.

- La Cour! Congratulations. What a breakthrough. And quite an ordeal, I hear. Pedersen said you looked a bit worse for wear. I'll refrain from asking what you were doing in Købmagergade in that attire, but it was just in time.

- Two of them got away.

- We'll find them. And you didn't expect to catch three at once and keep hold of them, did you? Good job, la Cour. Now we'll get them. We just need to get this one to sing a bit.

It turned out that the night's catch didn't exactly sing like a canary unless you included his extensive cock-and-bull repertoire.

8.

It was the task of the young magistrate Haack to interrogate what turned out to be waiter, Frederik Dalgaard Hansen, and it was quite an ordeal.

- Hansen, you lie through your teeth, and we know exactly who you are. Who did you share digs with at Istedgade 10?

- A young man named Smith.

- And that's another lie. Just like the description. Shall we do this again, Mr Hansen – the truth for once – just to try something new?

Hansen was also not very keen on revealing his current address, but that could be found out in other ways at least. Haack was very, very fed up with him.

Christian had more luck talking to waiter Hansen's colleagues at the Esplanade Pavilion. Hansen hadn't been there for long, but he was good at his job, although he was otherwise quite insufferable. Arrogant, self-assured, and to their surprise, the owner of several diamond rings, which he liked to flaunt. He had quickly become a topic of gossip among the staff. That sounded promising. More promising than the address Istedgade 10, which, according to the landlady, had been vacated long ago. As the lease was reportedly empty, Christian could go alone, which prompted some very serious considerations. Going to Istedgade wasn't a problem, but... could he get hold of Anna, and could he come up with an explanation for an invitation that wasn't too peculiar? From her side, there were no issues; she was a journalist and therefore, by definition, had a legitimate interest in anything related to the case. It was his own interest that was problematic. Would he have invited Bærentzen? No. Out of the question. So why invite Anna? Because. Because she was smart, with a waft of Jicky, and he hadn't been assigned a partner at the Detective Office yet, and he needed to talk, and... maybe she would notice something he didn't? 'What about the landlady?' That could be circumvented. Decision made. Fortunately, there was a telephone booth on Gammeltorv, so he could call Anna discreetly. And even more fortunately, she was at her desk and answered the phone immediately with an instant yes to join him at Istedgade right away.

Anna had already arrived when Christian showed up.

- Today's celebrated hero.

She laughed wholeheartedly.

- A rather battered one.

- Yes, I can see. Quite a mark you have on your face.

- I haven't had time to do anything about it. Come inside. We need to take a closer look at the delinquent's room. Just stay here while I talk to the landlady. She'll want explanations if she sees you, and your presence is none of her concern.

- I'm a journalist. My presence is perfectly natural.

- No, it's not, because nobody outside the police knows anything about this place yet. Wait.

Christian knocked on the landlady's door, who with a sour expression handed Christian a key and explained that they had moved out long ago.

- As I said, they ended the lease and left.

- I'll bring back the key when I'm done.

She shut the door with a slam of annoyance. Christian went down a floor and signalled to Anna, who cautiously came up the stairs. He nodded towards the door.

- It's in here.

Christian unlocked the door to a large room with an iron bed with two mattresses and a bedspread, a folding bed at the foot of the bed, an old writing desk with a mirror, a folding table two armchairs, a porcelain washbasin, a tall, old wardrobe, two windows facing the courtyard... and apparently completely stripped of anything that could be identified as personal belongings. Christian opened his bag, which Anna only noticed now. He took out some fine silk gloves and looked at Anna's hands. She was, as always, neatly dressed, which included fine kid leather gloves matching the hat, which today was a dark green trilby with pheasant feathers. Anna tried to recall the tour around Kronprinsensgade. No barging in, so she kept her composure in more ways than one. But everything had been cleaned after the move-out. Lifting mattresses and checking drawers didn't help. There wasn't even a specific smell – just dust and stuffiness and old furniture. The wardrobe was also empty except for two hangers. Christian attempted to reach into the hat shelf, which was above even his eye level. Nothing.

- There's nothing.

- Could you reach the back of the shelf?

Christian stood on tiptoe and reached his arm in as far as he could.

- No.

- Then help me with this.

Anna grabbed an armchair, which she tried to drag towards the wardrobe.

- Do you have a sheet of paper so I don't leave marks?

Christian took a sheet out of the bag, which Anna placed on the armrest.

- Hold it so it doesn't fall off.

She stepped onto the armrest and peered into the back of the shelf.

- There's something in there.

She reached as far as she could while Christian stood with his face in her skirt and held his breath.

- Look.

She held a small package in one hand and extended the other towards him in a way that clearly indicated he should hold it on the way down. Christian was handed the package – a small, neatly wrapped item in brown paper tied with thin twine. Before they could do more, the sound of footsteps came down the stairs. The chair's journey across the floor must have disturbed the landlady, and Anna was grateful that the door opened inward so she could quickly disappear behind it.

- Sorry, I had to move the chair. I hope I haven't disturbed you in anything important?

- Did you find anything?

- No.

- That's what I said. They moved out a month ago.

- Who were they?

- Hansen and his charming young friend Smith. He even gave me a photograph.

- Really? May I have a look?

- Of course. Just a moment.

The landlady went upstairs again, and Christian signalled for Anna to stay put. The landlady returned with a photograph of a young man.

- May I borrow it for the investigation, please?

- Yes, of course.

- I'll take one more look, then I'll come up with the key.

The landlady nodded and went back up, allowing Anna to emerge from behind the door. She looked at the photograph.

- Handsome young man. Smith? I doubt it.

- Me too. But we better lock up and move on. Unfortunately, I can't take you to the Central Bureau, so I can't show you the contents of the package. 5 o'clock?

- Tea and sandwiches?

Anna returned to the office with a wide smile, which was wiped off at the door just in case Bærentzen was there. There wasn't anything concrete to report yet, and she didn't want to be cross-examined about something she was sure could get Christian into trouble. Bærentzen wouldn't be able to keep quiet out of sheer excitement.

Christian went straight to Bugge and didn't need to hide a much broader smile as he placed the neat little parcel on the counter:

- Look, I'm bearing gifts. Well, one at least.

- Oooh. For me then?

Bugge untied the twine with a pair of tweezers. The brown paper was folded sharply, so it took some effort with the tweezers to fully unwrap the package. It turned out to be a real gift. Bugge spread out the papers – letters, telegrams, photos, and sketches of rooms were scattered over the counter and prompted a couple of appreciative whistles. One photo was identical to the one Christian had received from the landlady. And there was one where he was photographed with another young man. They looked almost identical except for their height.

What handsome young gentlemen. Let's see if they're anyone we know... is waiter Hansen finally talking?

- No. It's like pulling teeth. But maybe it'll help when he's presented with his friends – and plans? This sketch looks familiar.

- It must be above Møinichen's shop. Looks like a double win on this draw, la Cour. Madsen will be very pleased to see you.

That turned out to be an understatement. The relief at the Detective Office now being able to engage in more normal police work instead of being the post office for all the fingerprints of Europe was palpable. Even Commissioner Eugen Petersen showed up to express his satisfaction with the department as a whole and detective sergeant la Cour in particular. But the international aspect wasn't over yet and proved to be somewhat more challenging than expected.

There was still the question of waiter Hansen's current abode, and they finally succeeded in finding his lodgings in Borgergade. A boarding house similar to Istedgade. Christian had expected he had come into money – he had diamond rings – but it didn't look it. Maybe they hadn't sold anything yet? Right now, it would only lead to an immediate call to the police, almost no matter where or to whom he tried to sell them. Or maybe he just enjoyed wearing diamond rings? The room was furnished much like Istedgade. A bed, a table, a chair, a dresser, a wardrobe, a washbasin, and an armchair. There was some clothing – an extra waiter's outfit, extra collars, some underwear, simple collar studs, and socks but otherwise, almost no personal items. There was nothing to indicate he had a girlfriend, nothing relating to family or friends – nothing that could connect him to other people at all. There was nothing to read besides an old newspaper still lying on the table. He was a smoker – that much was clear. There was old cigar smoke in the air and three ashtrays. But... Christian sniffed – there was something else in the air besides tobacco. He looked closely at the ashtrays, where one of them looked like there wasn't just cigar ash but also something flaky – and the ashtray was sooty, as if a fire had been lit in it. He took his tweezers from his bag and prodded the ash a bit. Hansen had been burning paper, that was clear, but he had been careful and made sure there wasn't much left to read but a single letter of what Christian presumed was a letterhead. Hansen must have got nervous and removed anything that could relate him to other people or any kind of crime after all the attention with Møinichen.

The only suspicious thing was the diamond rings his colleagues were on about. The room looked completely normal for a man with a not very well-paid waiting job, who might occasionally get a good tip, so he could buy new shoes or – Christian looked at the dresser – a bottle of Floris Special No. 127, which must have cost a fortune. He opened the bottle and sniffed. Citrus, lavender, musk... He tried to remember the arrest. Hansen had smelled of sweat and cheap cigars – not even remotely floral, so it was probably only for special occasions, burglaries not included. Christian wondered why Hansen had been so unwilling to disclose the address when there was nothing to find. He went through the room again and took fingerprints from the ashtrays and the perfume bottle in case there were others than Hansen's own, but he didn't expect it.

Hansen had almost certainly been the only person in the room, and he had left nothing incriminating or personal. The landlady had recognised him from the police photo – otherwise, it would have been impossible to confirm it was him living there.

9.

Helena reported back that she had heard nothing about Leaning-Inger, and another visit to Schooner-Larsen's didn't yield any results either. She had simply vanished. It was a distraction that Christian had to address, as his instincts told him something was seriously wrong. Officially, he couldn't do much – he couldn't report her missing himself. He decided to go to Inger's room to see if he could find any clues as to her whereabouts.

Christian walked across the third courtyard to a building that looked like the next light snowfall would bring it crashing down. The journey from the street felt like a descent through the layers of society. The front building with its nice flats, shops, and sandstone decorations. The first rear building with smaller flats, workshops, and still fairly respectable residents, and last the far rear building and a courtyard overflowing with garbage and horse dung. With the outhouses, horse stables, sometimes pigs, and chickens, and where the dregs of society were crammed into microscopic flats or small rooms; in some places people lived in shifts – sleeping day or night as they could find work. There was no money to maintain any facade on neither the residents nor the house, which was made of old-fashioned half-timber – mud, straw, and horse manure. There wasn't much left of the railing on the gallery, and for a moment, Christian doubted if it would even hold his weight. The tenants of the rear buildings were usually small and emaciated and rarely grew larger than children. They were used to there being holes in everything and instinctively avoided dangerous places.

Inger lived in a room in the attic, which was probably originally meant as a drying loft. It had been divided with thin wooden walls lined with newspapers to create small rooms to let. Only half of them had a tiny oval window. Inger was one of the lucky ones. A little light came into her room. Christian remembered the time he had been there before on domestic, when her boyfriend had left her like a pile of trash on the floor and her screaming had been high enough to be noticed by others. Christian had carried her down and taken her to the hospital, where they had wrinkled their noses but patched her up again on his demand, and she had slept until her sailor boyfriend Peter had picked her up in an almost sober moment.

The door was only secured with a string around a nail, which Nielsen had probably tied to prevent it from rattling. There was no one in the room, which seemed deserted. But there was a strange smell on top of the usual stench of dung, dirt, cabbage, piss, and alcohol. Christian tried to distinguish the smells – the usual stench and then the additional layer of decay and rat droppings. He went in to find out where the smell came from, and it turned out to be from the room next door, where a sniff at a knothole in the wooden wall revealed that something had definitely died there, and it had been more than a couple of days ago. It also sounded like there were rats. Christian braced himself. It wasn't a sight he was looking forward to, but there was no way around it. He had to go in there. Already on the stairs, his nose had begun to protest, so he had expected something to be wrong.

The room next door was just as squalid as Inger's and almost completely dark. There was no small window and no other light sources besides small cracks between the bare roof tiles. But light wasn't necessary to be sure that someone had died. The stench was unbearable, and rats scurried around his legs as he entered. There seemed to be a long bundle on the floor. He grabbed a piece of cloth from a table and wrapped it round his hand before carefully lifting a corner of what looked like an old tarpaulin and held his breath. It could be Inger. Maybe.

He could do nothing now but get Nielsen back and have him come before someone complained about the stench, even though it wasn't much different from the odours already enveloping the building. The residents were pretty much immune.

Nielsen would ensure that Leaning-Inger ended up in forensics, and the Detective Office would receive a report and a murder case, which would probably be easy to solve once they found her boyfriend. He already had several convictions for violence. Christian had only seen him once, and it was one of the few times he'd had to knock a man out to protect himself.

*
**

Agnes got hold of her daughter while trying to look serious.

- Marie says, your policeman has been here several times?

- Yes. We work together. He is my source of all the stories about the jewel theft.

- And that's all?

- Actually, yes.

Anna got a look that indicated a severe lack of credibility.

- It's true. There's no... personal involvement what-soever. As I've explained, he can't have me as a guest at the Detective Office, where he sits for everyone to see, and I won't have Rasmussen or Bærentzen interfere under any circumstances.

Agnes was disappointed. There was an unfortunate likelihood that it was true, as Anna's enthusiasm for men – and marriage in particular – could fit on a very small space, say the top of a pin. The pointy end. And maybe the officer was spoken for.

- So be it. But if you end up... working closer together... make sure you take precautions?

- Yes.

Anna got annoyed. She knew her mother's hopes very well, and they were seriously misplaced, even though Christian's company suited her better than expected. With or without case files. And the irritating allusions were frankly misplaced. Especially as her mother used to speak her mind not only at home but also at the informal meetings, she held around the city, where you could learn more about family planning. Speaking of which. Maybe she should attend one of those meetings for some detective training. Could be an interesting clientele. But first, they had to attend a lecture by Karin Michaëlis on her new book: 'The Dangerous Age'. It was the talk of the town.

Christian and Bugge sat together at the Central Bureau examining the package Anna had found, apparently forgotten by waiter Hansen and his friend Smith, who wasn't really named Smith.

A closer inspection of the papers – especially the telegrams – showed that Hansen's roommate must be a Samuel Carstens, and there was another Carstens involved – a Hans Bernhard Carstens, living in England – there was even an address. They had discussed back and forth and planned various things, including the burglary at Møinichen's, judging by the drawing. It must also have been them caught in the act in Købmager-gade, and furthermore, they were planning a bank robbery. In the small town of Bogense, of all places. Carstens in London was supposed to procure some 'mechanics' for this purpose. There was cause for relief in Bogense – at least one thief was in custody. Another sounded like he had no intention of leaving London.

Now at least they knew who they were and could issue descriptions and photos: Samuel Johannes Carstens, 20 years old, 1.67 cm tall, fair hair with a middle parting, a crooked nose, thin eyebrows, slender, no moustache. Nicotine stains on the left hand. Hans Bernhardt Carstens, goes by the name of Carson, born in Stockton, England, 27 years old, 180 cm tall, upright, slim, agile, blond, curly hair, fresh complexion, blue eyes, athletic type. Probably back at his flat on Graven Street in London.

Now it was just a matter of waiting – and hoping.

Fingerprints showed it was indeed Leaning-Inger who lay in the bundle, and the autopsy report revealed that she had been strangled and subsequently or maybe simultaneously had her head banged into the wall. As Christian himself had expected, there was one suspect – Inger's boyfriend of several years, sailor Peter Anton Godtfredsen: Hot-tempered, unpredictable, and mostly dead drunk while on land. Nielsen was instructed to find him, and Madsen asked Christian to take Anders Strøm, who had just been given the desk opposite Christian's, to the crime scene for some field training.

Strøm was a nice bloke, fresh from the Jutland country-side, so Christian was curious as to how he would take it. He seemed like a placid type, and had proven to be perfect when things got heated – he almost radiated calm and composure. It also helped that he was two meters tall and as broad as a door. Christian hoped the stairs would hold his weight and thought they should go up separately. Together was simply too dangerous.

The stairs creaked ominously, as expected, when Strøm followed Christian. Christian had brought his bag, which Strøm, unlike the others, took an interest in. He had brought an extra torch so they could have a look around. There wasn't much to see except that a primus stove, which had been on a table, had ended up on the floor. Fortunately, it hadn't been lit. It had rolled a bit, hit the wall judging by the marks, and rolled back onto the floor, so it must have taken quite a hit. Christian put on gloves and put it in a cloth bag he had in his bag for that purpose.

- Needs to be tested for fingerprints,

he explained to Strøm. Otherwise, the place was so dirty that it would be futile to test anything.

Strøm looked around.

- You leave the countryside thinking it's better in the city, but there's no difference, really. In the rafters here or over the stables, it's all the same. Cold and squalid. Even the smell is almost the same, and the likelihood of getting beaten up too, I presume,

he philosophised, being more accustomed to the rural extremes of poverty.

They went into the room next door, from which Inger's body had been removed. With the help of the torches, it was possible to see the traces on the floor, left by someone dragging something from the door and then wrestling the tarpaulin. The dirt was scattered all around. Christian asked Strøm to look for blood-stains. They found them on the edge of the wooden wall by the door. So, the injuries were probably caused by dragging her around. Not attempted murder as such. There were still strands of hair in the dried blood, so Christian took out the tweezers, picked them out and put them in an envelope.

- So, what's your conclusion?

asked Christian as he took off the gloves and put them and the envelope in the bag. Strøm had taken notes along the way but didn't need to look at them yet.

- She probably argued with someone – both likely quite drunk; they got into a scuffle, which knocked the primus onto the floor. He grabbed her by the throat to shut her up – not necessarily to kill her. Then took the tarpaulin they had used as a blanket, wrapped her in it, and dragged her into the next room. She was too heavy for him – or he was just very drunk, so he banged her head on the wall on the way.

- Quite likely. Let's hope they find the sailor. And we'll have a chat with some of the other residents. Don't count on them having heard or seen anything, but you never know.

It turned out Strøm had the same talent for looking nice and approachable and being just the right person to confide in, as Christian did himself, but there wasn't much to confide from the three women they met in the courtyard. No, they hadn't seen or heard anything other than the usual noise of screaming kids and arguments and rat-arsed men coming home and mistaking the dunny, the door, or the girlfriend. Nothing had been different in the last couple of days. They hadn't seen much of Inger, but they weren't used to – she was a night owl, they said with knowing looks, and the sailor had supposedly been there but had disappeared again. Nothing mysterious about that either – he was a sailor. What'd you expect?

On the way back to the office, Christian gave Bugge the primus stove, which was the only thing that might have fingerprints. He wondered if the murder of Leaning-Inger was just a coincidence, or if she had some connection to the jewel theft. She probably hadn't been near the jewellery, but could she have seen something? Or was he just being too fanciful?

Both Christian and Strøm attended Inger's funeral, where a few others had also turned up and squinted uncomfortably in a daylight they weren't used to, but they came. The priest from the hospital chapel was a sensible man who kept his eulogy short and focused on the forgiveness of sins. Something today's audience appreciated instead of the usual and absolutely ineffective admonishments they were accustomed to. There was still no word on Osvaldo, and still nothing particularly mysterious about that.

Christian and Strøm went back to the office, where Madsen smiled to himself. They were an odd couple but they seemed to get along well and had mutual respect. Both different, and both intelligent, attentive, and with a natural ability to treat everyone kindly and without prejudice. They would make a good team. Madsen had placed Strømmen, as they already called him, in exactly the right place.

Anna's day brought a story for the paper that might be the answer to a puzzle that had been talked about for several years, and with a bit of luck, it would also have a sequel when confirmed. In the summer of 1897, three Swedes took off from Spitsbergen in a balloon aiming to fly over the North Pole. Since then, no one had heard from them. Chief engineer Andrée was convinced that a balloon trip could yield new scientific discoveries, and Fænkel and Strindberg had joined him – convinced of the same. Some time ago, a telegram had arrived from the Swedish consulate in Montreal, stating that the remains of the balloon had been found. Now, a Catholic bishop at a conference in Toronto had come forward with a story. He had been on a visitation trip and had spoken with a missionary in Saskatchewan who had travelled north, where the locals talked about a house that had fallen from the sky. They had gone hunting, and when they had seen the missionary's revolver, they had said that 'the white men' also had one. They explained that 'a large white house covered with ropes' had fallen down, in which three white men lived. They had died shortly after. Since then, the locals had gone to the 'house' when they needed rope, because there was so much of it.

Polar expeditions always made good stories, and sometimes even scandals, like with Cook, who received a hero's welcome until it became clear that he probably hadn't been to the North Pole at all. In a few months, Knud Rasmussen would leave for an expedition that might cast light on the matter.

10.

Karin Michaëlis' lecture on women's dangerous age hadn't been widely advertised, but that had no effect on neither the buzz nor the attendance. The lecture hall was filled with expectant women, looking forward to an evening that was bound to be scandalous, and where it could be just as interesting to see who else showed up as it was to see the author. When the intermission was announced, there was an eager chatter, and Anna and her mother shared in the excitement, scanning the crowd for familiar faces just like everyone else. There was only one face Anna recognised, and she absolutely hadn't expected to see it at this event. Christian was here and he made a beeline for her.

- How did you know I was here?
- Where else would you be?

Christian grinned. He hadn't doubted for a second that Anna would be at a lecture the entire city was talking about, with a scandalous woman set to speak about her equally scandalous book. As he looked up, he spotted Helena, who also spotted him. He glanced around and also saw his mother, who also saw him – and laughed. In a second, he was surrounded by Anna, Anna's mother Agnes, who had been standing next to Anna the whole time, unbeknownst to him, his own mother Ida – and Helena. And everyone would expect to be introduced, as they had seen him talking to Anna.

For the first time in his life, Christian felt discomfited in female company. But only for a moment. Anna took the lead:

- Mum, meet detective Christian la Cour, whose visits you are so concerned about. Christian, this is my mother, Dr Agnes Lendorph.

Christian greeted Agnes Lendorph, a middle-aged woman in tweed with greying chestnut hair and grey-blue eyes, who seemed to have noticed everything and analysed his innermost thoughts several times over before he even extended his hand. But there was also a glint in her eye that reminded him of his own mother's, suggesting a similar sense of humour.

- How do you do, Dr Lendorph... Uh, Mum, meet journalist Anna Lendorph from Aftenbladet, whom I've mentioned. Anna – my mother Ida la Cour.

Anna greeted Ida – a slender, graceful woman, as dark as Christian, with quick movements, high spirits, and a permanent twinkle in her eye. She looked like she would be a fun acquaintance. Helena tilted her head and locked eyes with Christian with a 'so, what's your next move, cheeky boy?' expression, which the other three women followed and expectantly understood, while they guessed – and guessed quite correctly – at her profession. Helena noted that there was not a hint of prejudice from anyone; only welcoming, very curious attention.

- Anna, meet Helena Wittgens, whom I got to know while I was at Nørrebro. Helena – Anna, whom I've told about, my mother Ida, and Dr Lendorph.

Christian gained silent respect all around, as the women now greeted each other and almost in unison thought, 'well handled and – interesting. This needs following up.' And Christian thought, 'well, this is going quite well, so why not go the whole mile?' He couldn't stay without attracting considerable attention in a way that could cause problems elsewhere, and he needed to make an appointment. That was his reason for being there. So, he ended the meeting with a

- Anna, can we meet at yours tomorrow morning? There's a case that might be connected to the jewel case that I'd like to discuss. If Helena can come too?

- Of course. Kronprinsessegade 26b, first floor, Helena. And you'd better keep a low profile, Christian, unless you want to feature in my colleagues' reports from this meeting. There's already one heading this way.

Christian nodded to the ladies and melted away. Fortunately – perhaps – for the ladies, the intermission was over, and it was time to find their seats again. And so, they did. Without exception, determined to meet again at the earliest opportunity. For Ida la Cour, it meant four new names on the guest list for the next party. She assumed there was also a Mr Lendorph, probably Professor Lendorph, but almost certainly no Mr Wittgens. 'I wonder if any of my usual guests have met Miss Wittgens before?' All likelihood pointed towards it. Ida was close to bursting out laughing at the thought. 'Maybe it should be a masquerade?'

Back home, Anna and Agnes had a cup of tea and a chat about the evening's lecture, inevitably also touching on the unexpected rendezvous.

- So, that's your detective. My goodness, he's handsome. You didn't mention that. I think I've seen his mother on stage. If I remember correctly, she can kick the hat off a man and hit a note even higher. And the la Cours are famous for their parties, even I've heard about them.

- Maybe we'll be invited next time?

- And Helena. Had you heard of her?

- No. Not a word. But we haven't actually talked about anything other than the jewel case. Until now.

- Intelligent woman, I'm sure. I'd like to talk to her. Please invite her for tea – or to one of my meetings. The next one is on Wednesday.

- I shall.

It was Christian who arrived first, so Anna had the opportunity to ask who Helena was. Christian explained how he had found her as a crumpled-up victim in the midst of being murdered, and how he had knocked the would be killer to the ground and restrained him. How he had carried Helena to the hospital, where they almost refused to attend to her, and how he had later ensured she got new bandages, medication, and something to eat. Since then, she had blossomed and was now a 'self-employed businesswoman' – Anna could hear the air quotes – and was doing quite well. Christian described the premises including a splendid not to say opulent boudoir in purple silk and velvet frequented by the city's most respectable pillars of society. He visited regularly – for conversation, of course – about all sorts of things because they both needed a friend who was completely outside of everyday life, yet somehow not entirely. The explanation ended with stories of Limping-Arnold, the Professor, Dirty-Mie, Captain Olsen, and Osvaldo, and a few more from the lower levels of society Christian had encountered at Nørrebro, either arresting them, helping them home to bed, or rescuing them from an even bigger crook. He was friendly with most of them. Perhaps because he also cared about them and didn't just let people die, Anna thought.

He told about Leaning-Inger, who was always so drunk she had to lean on something including in the physical sense, preferably a man with money for more brandy, and who was now murdered, and how it was likely her equally drunken sailor boyfriend was the murderer. But there was something nagging him, and that's why he had asked to meet – and to involve Helena. She arrived as she was mentioned, and was invited in for tea.

- It's about Leaning-Inger, isn't it?

she asked as she took off her coat.

- Yes. We're still looking for Peter, her boyfriend, but there's something about this that feels off. I can't help but think it might have something to do with the jewel thefts. He's had so many opportunities to kill her over the years, so why now? And why dump her in the next room? When he's drunk and goes berserk, he's incoherent and wouldn't be able to think that far. Not wrap her in a tarp either. It doesn't make sense.

Anna and Helena listened to Christian's explanation of how he had found her, and how he and Strømmen had returned to her place officially. About the results from the autopsy and the funeral and the nagging feeling of having overlooked something. A feeling of wrongness he couldn't explain but just respond to. Did they understand? They both laughed and declared that, for once, a man was equipped with intuition, an excellent quality for a detective, and what did he want them to do? Could they possibly talk to the residents of the house? There were always women there, and they kept an eye on each other so therefore also on all sorts of other things, but they had seen him before, and he was the police, so it was unlikely they would tell him anything. He and Strømmen hadn't made a big deal of talking to anyone when they picked up Inger – partly because they didn't think it would lead to anything other than the expected – Inger and Peter had been drunk as usual – and partly because most had just melted into the background when they showed up. Being in plain clothes hadn't made a difference. They were strangers – that was enough.

- But so are we?

- Yes, but you're women and therefore not someone immediately perceived as a threat, and it's out of the question you're police and thus in any risk of completely inadvertently stumble upon things, such as something that fell out of someone else's pocket, entirely by chance, I swear, I found it on the street, officer.

Christian played the role of a completely innocent pickpocket to perfection.

- If you stick together, it's even more unlikely you're snoops. You just took a wrong turn, and we thought Madame Stoltze lived here, but maybe you know someone else who sells drops?

- What are you hoping to find out?

- If anyone else has been visiting. If Peter has been home recently. If they have seen any strangers in the house at any time in the past week or before. If Inger behaved normally – said anything, hinted at anything about seeing something, knowing something, meeting someone... She might not have kept it to herself.

Anna and Helena looked at each other. Christian's explanation made sense, and no one should get away with murder, so there was no hesitation as they nodded at each other.

- It's a deal,

they said almost in unison. And laughed.

- Will you make your own arrangements? I have to get back to the office before anyone asks for me.

Christian left the ladies, who continued to drink tea.

- I have an invitation from my mother – for tea, or if you'd rather come to an informal meeting for women on Wednesday.

- A meeting?

- My mother holds small meetings on family planning around the city. She – and I – believe it's a woman's right to be the master of her own body, especially in regard to having children. So, she advises as much as she can. It's perfectly legal and so are the remedies – we're considerably luckier than women in other countries – but you're not allowed to advertise.

Helena smiled.

- We can definitely find something to talk about. I know most of the remedies and sell some of them to my highly esteemed customers and colleagues and quite discreetly. I import them myself from France.

They agreed it might be easier to find a time for tea that didn't disrupt Helena's business, and that the next morning would be a good time to visit Inger's abode. Helena looked up at the foils on the wall.

- In case you run out of arguments?

- Nah, I've got a Schouboe.

Helena laughed.

- Much more efficient and easier to have in a handbag, although I think it's tough on the lining.

Anna laughed back.

- It's actually a real problem. Christian suggested a small Webley.

- That's my choice too. Shall I get you one? One of my customers is a dealer.

- Yes, please do. I hate it when my handbag goes out of shape.

- Deal. But I have to go now. I'm looking forward to tomorrow.

- Me too.

Helena walked home thinking that Christian had won the marriage lottery if he played his cards right, which he seemed to be doing. She, like his mother, had been worried since Ingeborg had left for America, because of his peculiar taste in women – he preferred them independent and intelligent. And Anna would be lucky if she refrained from resisting longer than absolutely necessary. Christian would never ask her to be anything other than herself or try to control her. Never take her for granted and treat her like a piece of the furniture. Or spend her money on gambling. She was interested – Helena was sure of that. She just didn't know it yet, and she had no doubt marriage wasn't on Anna's to-do list. It wasn't on Helena's either.

Anna put on her hat and coat to go to the office and find some interesting stories for tomorrow.

The expanded police cooperation bore fruit, and word came from the Royal Danish Legation in Berlin that the German police had arrested Samuel Carstens in Hamburg, and that he was now in Kiel. They would extradite him if the Danish police arrived in Kiel as soon as possible with proper documentation to pick up the detainee.

The relief at the Detective Office was considerable, and it was immediately decided that Schou and la Cour should leave at once. Both were intimately familiar with the case, and both spoke German. And, if Carstens proved difficult and only wanted to speak English, la Cour could handle that too.

Only three hours later, they were on the train to Korsør, and telegrams had been sent to Hamburg and Kiel about their arrival. Christian didn't even have time to inform Anna, and although he was proud of being chosen for the trip, there was also the matter of Inger, which still haunted him, and he was more than curious to hear how the new detective duo of Anna and Helena was doing. But that would have to wait. Right now, one of the most wanted burglars in Europe was to be picked up in Kiel and escorted to Copenhagen.

Now, only one culprit was missing, and they could hope that Scotland Yard would live up to expectations. They were fairly certain that Hans Carstens had returned to London. The question was, how good he was at hiding.

The time of miracles continued into the afternoon when a telegram arrived from the Danish Consulate in London, stating that Hans Bernhard Carstens had been arrested at his home – he simply hadn't anticipated any need to hide. Scotland Yard had expected his brother Samuel to show up within a few days, but caution and Hans Carstens's behaviour had led them to arrest him now. They would hold him for up to a week while awaiting evidence from Copenhagen as the basis for extradition. Hans Carstens was born in England and therefore a British citizen, so it was only just possible to extradite him; not as straightforward as with his brother, who was born in Denmark.

Copenhagen replied they should not expect to see anything of Samuel Carstens as his itinerary had been changed from London to Copenhagen, curtesy of the Hamburg constabulary. They had chosen to guard the train station after a telegram from Copenhagen and could therefore pick up Carstens as he arrived and ensure accommodation for him at the local jail.

On the train to Korsør, Schou and Christian had to restrain themselves from discussing the case, even though they both very much wanted to. They weren't alone in the compartment, and it was out of the question to do anything but small talk. Or just remain silent, which quickly became the decision, so they didn't get on each other's nerves with trivialities.

It wasn't until they were on the ferry to Kiel that they had the opportunity to talk, as they had been allowed to use the captain's cabin. He even came himself after just an hour's sailing and told them he had received a telegram from Assistant Commissioner Madsen: The other Carstens brother had been arrested in London. Madsen believed they deserved to get that news right away. It was a good trip to Kiel.

The journey back was more difficult, as Samuel Carstens was not at all pleased, and even though he was a small man, he was handcuffed to both Schou and Christian. The police had delivered them to the steamer and the captain's cabin. The trip on the train from

Korsør was uncomfortable – they had to stay in the mail waggon, which wasn't set up for passengers, as it wasn't possible to lock a regular compartment.

Christian used the journey to take a good look at Carstens and try to remember if he could recognise him from Købmagergade. He couldn't. It had been too dark, and Carstens had run too fast. But he could remember his smell and was sure it was this Carstens who had pushed him down the stairs.

Carstens didn't say a word and would clearly be a challenge for assessor Haack, who would have to get a confession out of him to secure a conviction. Christian was sure he would succeed, but it might take time and would require further evidence or witnesses. Christian's sense of smell would not be sufficient evidence to secure a conviction for Købmagergade and certainly not for Møinichen.

While Christian was in Kiel, Anna and Helena were on a backyard excursion, both disguised, i.e., wearing clothes they had struggled to find. Both were fashion-conscious and only wore bespoke, and neither of them held onto old clothes. Anna had been helped by Marie, who had lent her a hat and a skirt, and Helena had visited a pawnshop. Together, the two ladies resembled women attempting to look above their station, which was precisely the intention, and armed with baskets, they could pretend to be on a shopping spree which had gone astray in search of some more dubious 'medicine'. Further specification hopefully wouldn't be necessary.

They entered the backyard, where there were definitely stares, but no one was in a hurry to disappear. Two women with shopping baskets pose no threat. They stood for a moment waiting for their noses to shut down from a stink, strong enough to sting the eyes. The plan was to inquire about the non-existent Madam Stoltze, and when no one knew who she was, if perhaps Inger knew her, and if Inger was at home, etc.

It worked reasonably well until they wanted to know more about Inger. There was no suspicion in the air, but no one had seen her in over a week, maybe two, but Helena somehow managed to corral the women of the house together so they could supplement each other and start discussing Inger in general and visiting strangers in particular.

After much deliberation, the ladies agreed that no; they hadn't seen Inger recently, nor her sailor boyfriend Peter, but that wasn't so strange. He usually – if at all – came at mealtimes, i.e., when they were all busy peeling potatoes or cooking cabbage or gruel, and thus not paying attention to neither stairs nor yard.

But there had apparently been a man they had never seen before. Five days ago – seven maybe? No precise agreement here, nor on the man's appearance. He had just been different; foreign, better dressed – perhaps waiter-like in style – black clothes and no hat. Had he gone up? No conclusion there either. No one had been close to him, and he hadn't said anything to anyone, or wait a minute? Didn't he ask Jeppe about Inger?

After a brief discussion about whether said Jeppe was even nearby or could have been, Jeppe was called for, and he ambled over and confirmed that yes, there had been a man who had asked about Leaning-Inger and had been shown her lodgings upstairs and had gone up there without so much as a thank you or a coin. Jeppe was outraged – it wasn't just bad form, it was completely unheard of when said person obviously had money – he had a gold ring with a shiny stone, and should therefore be able to follow conventions.

Jeppe's explanation was followed by an indignant spit ball. Anna and Helena understood a subtle hint, and Anna fished a coin out of her pocket for Jeppe, who promptly disappeared. They thanked the ladies for their help and bid farewell, explaining that they were going to look for Madam Stoltze elsewhere. It seemed Christian's hunch could be right. Maybe it wasn't Peter who had killed Inger. Maybe it was someone else.

Anna went home to change her clothes and tried to call Christian. She was informed that he was travelling on official business and wouldn't be in the office until the next day. Anna had to arm herself with patience she absolutely did not possess and went to her desk at the newsroom to find fresh stories from abroad. There was plenty to choose from.

The choice fell on a solved double murder in Sweden. An elderly couple had been found dead in bed in Leksand in Dalarna, and it was first thought that they had died of smoke inhalation until a labourer confessed that he and two accomplices had poisoned them by giving them coffee with arsenic before setting fire to the house. When they had screamed, the perpetrators had stuffed handkerchiefs into their mouths to stop the screams. That was what they had died from before the arsenic had taken effect – or the fire.

If Copenhagen didn't offer sufficient drama, one had to borrow. It turned out later in the day that it wasn't necessary at all.

The evening brought a completely unexpected local drama. At seven o'clock, a neatly dressed gentleman had walked down Hindegade. He had suddenly stopped, pulled a revolver out of his pocket, and shot himself twice in the head. With blood streaming down his face, he had collapsed and hit a little boy just passing by. An ambulance was immediately called, which took the man to Frederik's Hospital. No name, no papers, nothing that in any way suggested who he was. He had only said a couple of words in the ambulance, believed to be in English, and turned out to be tattooed all over his chest.

Christian barely managed to deliver Carstens to the station before he was called to the hospital to see if he could possibly offer any insight into who it might be – and if there was any connection to the robberies. Other officers had been called, not recognising the man, and he didn't appear anywhere in the Central Bureau's records. The English words he had spoken were unrecognisable in the form they were relayed to Christian. He didn't dare guess what it was about. A letter was sent to London with description, photo, and fingerprints. The morning papers called him 'an English sailor.'

11.

The police's next statement to the press came with great fanfare: All three suspected perpetrators of the attempted robbery at Rungwald were now in custody; two in Copenhagen, one extradited from Kiel; efforts were made to extradite the third from London. The press busied themselves playing detectives as names finally emerged, sparking intense competition.

Meanwhile, assessor Haack struggled to extract anything from the delinquents, a far more challenging task. At the Foreign Office, the process of extraditing Hans Bernhard Carstens began with the first telegram from London, stating they had a week to gather evidence satisfactory to the English legal system. Usually, there wasn't much enthusiasm for sending citizens abroad, regardless of their alleged crimes, so the Foreign Ministry urged prompt action. The statements of the two detainees in Denmark couldn't be used as evidence unless sworn under oath, a practice not used in Denmark.

Further inquiries into Samuel Carstens whereabouts, shared by the police, revealed that a railway worker had identified him from a photograph, confirming his journey to Hamburg by night train right after the robbery.

The sleepy village of Ballerup suddenly found itself swarmed by journalists upon learning that the Carstens brothers had spent their summer holiday there in the company of their mother. They had lodged with a local photographer Hansen, who professed ignorance of any suspicious activity involving the two well-groomed young men or their mother. Yes, they travelled around, including trips by train and taxi to Copenhagen, but wasn't that quite common? Almost every villager, down to every child and dog, was interrogated, but no interesting stories emerged. The Carstens family had apparently taken a completely normal summer holiday.

Hotel Bristol became the next focus of attention. At least one Carstens brother had stayed there, namely Hans Bernhard Carstens from London. At a particularly incriminating time. And it wasn't the first time either. Anna had spent more time poring over the guest book at Hotel Bristol than her colleagues, and there she had stumbled upon a scoop that she could hardly wait to share with Christian, whom she intended to inform before he could read it in the paper. It was urgent. He probably wouldn't be thrilled, but at least he could be prepared if a woman suddenly appeared in the case. She chuckled to herself as she waited for him.

Upon his arrival, he was settled into an armchair with a beer and a sandwich and warned not to choke on either in a moment. Christian began eating his ham-and-cheese sandwich in bemusement while Anna nearly giggled, a sight he had never seen before. He was eager to hear what she found so amusing – and to come with a warning. Anna started her explanation, which had the expected effect.

- There's also a sister Carstens.

- No way!

- Oh yes. Hans Carstens stayed at Hotel Bristol with their sister, where he assumed the identity of plantation owner Carstens from Brazil. They spent their time in Copenhagen robbing jewellers in a not so spectacular way.

- Plantation owner? From Brazil?

- Exactly. Big man, big spender, big everything. And, above all, a big thief, though he left the actual thievery to his sister during their grand tour of the city. Where they got caught.

- But why aren't they behind bars then?

- Because it was when Alberti was Minister of Justice, and Carstens wrote to him personally, expressing deep regret that his poor sister, who was a kleptomaniac and therefore absolutely couldn't help herself – it was terribly sad – unfortunately had been helping herself at various jewellers, and whether there could be a discreet arrangement for him to simply take the poor girl back to Brazil? Where she would be well taken care of. Carstens later referred to Alberti as his very good friend and praised him highly.

- You're making it up!

- Nope. Alberti felt sorry for the poor girl, so she was immediately pardoned, and Carstens was allowed to pick her up, after which they sensibly hurried to leave. For New York. I doubt either of them has ever been to Brazil. However, Hans has definitely been to both Chicago and Toronto.

- You don't say.

- That's exactly what I'm saying. With a very successful career as a safecracker. Completely official and legitimate. He even won a competition in Chicago for the fastest safe opening – with dynamite.

Christian, as expected, nearly choked on his sand-wich.

- Say that again. He won a competition for opening safes with dynamite?

- Indeed.

- In Chicago?

Yes, detective, sir. In Chicago. Then he got more orders to open safes in banks and other places where the owner had died. He actually lived there for a couple of years and had a very profitable business. As for why he then went to Canada, the story doesn't say – I believe he just saw a business opportunity, or someone approached him.

- Where?

- Toronto. After the big fire, there were both banks and private residences where safes had been damaged and therefore couldn't be opened in the usual way. So, he made quite a bit of money being very good at opening safes with dynamite there as well. And with no side business, as far as is known. Not in Chicago either. Although it might seem a bit suspicious that he didn't stay in Toronto and didn't return to Chicago either. But maybe there were no more unopened safes.

- Well, no wonder then he knew the recipe for a bank robbery in Bogense and had 'the mechanics'. I wonder if Scotland Yard knows? ... Is she really their sister?

- I don't know. Could be, but she's disappeared and wasn't on holiday in Ballerup either. It might just as well have been a female acquaintance in the same line of work, who may have stayed behind in New York.

- At least there were no traces of a woman at Møinichen's, and only men came down the stairs at Rungwald's.

- Maybe a woman would be smart enough to go up the stairs instead and just stay quiet until everyone had run away? You ran too, didn't you?

Christian looked almost panicked. Then he closed his eyes and tried to think.

- I was at Møinichen's not long after, and no one else had been there. There was no trace of a woman. No fingerprints. No footprints. No clothing marks. No scent. At Rungwald's, I arrived in the midst of it all, and there was nothing to indicate that there was a woman nearby. No sound of anyone running up, no scent – nothing. There's also nothing in the various letters and telegrams to suggest that any other than the waiter and the two Carstens brothers are involved.

- Sorry. But it could have happened, couldn't it?

- Yes – in theory. But I would have noticed.

They allowed themselves some time to eat in silence. But there was also Inger. Anna told him about the trip with Helena, and Christian had no doubt that she had enjoyed every second of it. He thought she could be a fantastic colleague if the police weren't so old-fashioned. Foolish, considering that women could talk to other women in a way that men – and the police especially – could never do.

- So, the boy saw someone who sounds like waiter Hansen – ring and all – asking for Inger. A much better result than Strømmen and I could have achieved. I'll have to follow up on that. Maybe we should take a trip to the Esplanade Pavilion? What do you say?

- If we can find a time of day when his colleagues have time for a chat?

- Should be possible. May I invite you for coffee, Miss Lendorph?

- Thank you, gladly, Mr la Cour.

Anna tilted her head and winked at him.

- What about the English sailor?

- No one knows who he is, and judging by the tattoos, he is probably English. We've sent prints and photographs. The clothing absolutely doesn't match that of a sailor, but the tattoos do. There's something not quite right, but hopefully it's Scotland Yard's problem, not ours. There's no doubt that he shot himself, so we don't need to look for a culprit, but can close the case here.

- Well, that's something, at least.

The Esplanade Pavilion was a charming place, especially popular for their Sunday afternoon dances. Earlier on Sundays, it was open but nearly empty, and Anna and Christian got a window table where the waiter was attentive and had plenty of time. There were no other guests, and he was clearly bored. He didn't recognise Christian as the detective who had questioned them about Hansen, and if Anna did the talking, he possibly wouldn't even remember hearing Christian's voice before, if he noticed that sort of thing at all. Probably too many voices to keep track of.

Anna chatted away – the story had been in the papers, so everyone knew waiter Hansen had worked there. She mentioned, of course, that it must have been shocking for everyone, to which the waiter allowed himself a little smile and remarked that perhaps it didn't come as such a terrible surprise to them.

- He had these diamond rings, you see. Quite unusual for a waiter.

- Really? No, I've never heard of such a thing before. And several, you say?

- Yes, at least three different ones. And it was hard not to notice because he had a habit of catching the light with the diamonds when there were no guests and he was bored. I don't think he noticed himself, but it does catch attention when light spots dart around the walls.

- That must have looked funny. But I thought you were here in pairs, so you could chat?

- Yeah, but someone's got to do the work, even though you can chat while doing the chores.

- Or maybe get a visit from the girlfriend?

Anna gave him a mischievous look.

- Yeah...

The waiter chuckled.

- It happens. Although I'm not sure they were all girlfriends. Anna looked questioningly at the waiter, who was happy to go on.

- Hopefully the last one Hansen had come visit wasn't his girlfriend. She was a strange one and no mistake. Dirty clothes and smelled of grog. He looked completely taken aback when she showed up and he wanted rid of her. But she wouldn't leave unless he went with her. He managed in the end – maybe he gave her some money. Seemed a bit odd afterwards – dropped a glass. Never saw that before. But it's a good thing she disappeared – she would have scared away all the other customers. Strange girl.

- Maybe they'd met in town, and she had designs on him?

Anna suggested.

- Maybe. But thankfully we haven't seen her since.

Christian was fascinated by Anna's efficient interviewing technique, which really wasn't all that different from his own.

A new couple entered the cafe, so the waiter excused himself. They had enough coffee and cake on the table, anyway. Anna and Christian looked at each other. Maybe it was Inger visiting, but it was a bit difficult to ask about her appearance without arousing suspicion. Maybe it would be necessary to interrogate the waiters properly, but how? Hansen was arrested in connection with the jewel thefts, and there was nothing else to suggest that Inger had anything to do with it; she was dead and buried, and the case was closed.

- Have you searched Hansen's lodgings?

- I went there myself, but that was before I heard about Inger. ... Maybe it's worth going back there again...

- Tomorrow? Where?

- Borgergade. Shall we meet at the Gothersgade end?

Anna smiled, satisfied. That was exactly what she had been angling for.

- Good idea.

They continued chatting about nothing and every-thing. Anna would have liked to ask about Helena, but she had a feeling she wouldn't get an answer for the simple reason that Christian would think she should ask Helena herself. Instead, she asked about Leaning-Inger, who could no longer answer anyone, and Christian explained she had been a regular part of his life at Nørrebro police station, where she was often picked up at night and carried to the detention, unable to walk herself due to alcohol – or more likely – alcohol and beatings, because she could become very aggressive and malicious when she needed more brandy and had no money.

Not all men had the patience to wait for her to leave on her own accord – and they usually ended up waiting in vain, anyway. Those who knew her gave her a smack, so she fell down and left them alone. And then it was up to the next officer on the beat to pick her up. Some just leaned her against the nearest house wall – others took her the short way to the station. Christian always took her with him, he explained. If nothing else, she got a roof over her head and a warm blanket – more than she had at home – and a roll for breakfast – also more than at home. And – and this was very unofficial – usually a shot or two from the bottle in the drawer for this specific purpose, so she wouldn't suffer such violent withdrawal symptoms that she screamed the house down and disturbed the whole neighbourhood, including any officer on duty in need of a snooze.

Otherwise, she was a regular fixture at the small dives on the second and third floors, was a nice person when she wasn't in need, and usually gave to others if she could – including a comforting word and a dirty handkerchief to comrades if they had experienced something distressing and needed a shoulder to cry on. That was why one of the pub landlords had reached out to Christian when she suddenly disappeared, even though it was with some risk to himself. He had no idea about her livelihood – maybe washing, maybe begging, maybe prostitution and a little pick-pocketing when she wasn't too drunk. Maybe all of it in turn.

- By the way, my mother asked for your address,

Christian suddenly burst out and explained it was for invitations to the next party.

- You – and your mother, for that matter – must really have made an impression. She was very insistent. The invitation is for both you and your parents. You seemed to get along fine at the lecture.

Anna explained that they certainly did, and her mother had heard about his mother's famous parties and hoped to be invited, so she could confidently expect a yes from all three of them.

- Is Helena invited too?

- Yes indeed. And she said yes.

Anna and Christian looked each other in the eye and thought the same thing – 'does she know any of the other guests' – and laughed simultaneously, knowing it was for exactly the same reason.

- My mother said she's seen your mother dance. Could that be true?

- Easily. She's danced on all the variety stages in Copenhagen, so it would be pretty strange if she hadn't.

Christian looked at Anna. Then he took out his wallet and pulled out a photograph of a woman in a sequined dancing costume and a little boy about four years old, both with a leg in the air in a theatre dressing room. Her foot was next to her head – he reached to his belly button, and he clearly had to hold her hand to keep from toppling over in his enthusiasm to do a high kick like his mother.

Christian handed the picture to Anna, who looked at it, then at Christian, and back at the picture, smiling at it.

- You're delightful. I assume you can kick just as high as your mother now?

She looked up at him again.

- Yes. And my mother can still kick the hat off a man.

There was pride in his voice. And love. No doubt the little Christian had had fun with his mother, and the theatre had got hold of him from a very early age. Maybe he had been with them before he could walk. He read her thoughts.

- I went with them from the time I could be taken in a basket. My father had no objections. He thought I should be with my mother and not a nanny in an otherwise empty flat, because he came along too. So, in the evenings, I was looked after by my father in my mother's dressing room and spoiled rotten by absolutely everyone at the theatre.

- I can understand that. You must have been utterly irresistible. So, that's why you became a dancer? You've – quite literally – got dance and theatre with your mother's milk?

- Yes, of course. And I was lucky enough to meet Bournonville, who made sure there were wonderful parts for the men. I loved it.

The intimate atmosphere was interrupted by the waiter, who came back to ask if he could be of more help, but it was getting time to break up and move on to the rest of the Sunday appointments – at least for

Anna. Christian put the photograph back in his wallet, got the bill, paid, and they parted ways at Kronprinses-segade, where Christian said a polite goodbye at the gate. Anna almost danced up the stairs at the thought of tomorrow's detective work, and Christian walked home, happy that tomorrow would bring more Anna. Later, Anna had lunch with her parents and two generations Bohr before heading to the fencing club.

Neither waiter Hansen nor Samuel Carstens showed any more cooperation in the subsequent interrogations with assessor Haack, but it didn't make much difference compared to the hassle with Carstens in London. It turned into a very long and very sharp correspondence between the Danish consulate and the court in London, which blankly refused to acknowledge the evidence presented in the case. Madsen and the Commissioner cursed in unison with the lawyers from the Ministry of Foreign Affairs and agreed that it was pure malevolent obstruction from the London court.

There was an ancient extradition agreement, but it was not up to par with the new reality of international crime, fingerprints, etc. The case was adjourned for a few days at a time while London waited for what they perceived as evidence – including those that simply could not exist – such as sworn statements from the other detainees.

Madsen read from a telegram: 'After perusing last night, the judge today unequivocally stated that under

English law, there was not an iota of evidence, not even a scintilla of evidence. Yet the case was adjourned for the last time.'

It didn't help that the London court went into nitpicking differences between 'housebreaking' and 'shopbreaking', which could get interesting, as the shop was located in a residential building and the burglars went through an office to gain access.

The opinion at the Detective Office was that in London, obstacles were deliberately created because they did not want to extradite Carstens, but also did not want to say this directly, probably because they would have to come up with a reason.

There were speculations that the police in London were busy figuring out whether Carstens could be involved in criminal activity in England, and did not want anyone to obtain information about this through the extradition case. That was the only reasonable scenario imaginable, but there were ways to convey this that would not be recorded, and they had not used them. The diplomatic exchange became increasingly icy.

Anna went to the newsroom and had a chat with Bærentzen about the case – including the English reluctance to extradite Carstens and the attempt to come up with a sensible explanation as to why.

Bærentzen was thrilled by the stories about the sister and the connection to Alberti and especially the story about 'the safe opener Carstens' and his merits in Chicago and Toronto. It was bold, it was fun, and it was front page. It couldn't get much better.

Anna decided maybe it could if she could get hold of her great-uncle, who must have heard about the case, and who could at least ensure access to the court in London, and who should also have some contacts in the police who could provide something new. She decided to send a telegram to Windlesham to inquire if Uncle Arthur was at home – or even better – in London. As soon as she had visited Hansen's lodgings with Christian.

Christian and Anna met as planned, and there was a bit to walk along Borgergade, and thus time to talk about the case.

Christian talked about the shopbreaking/house-breaking issue – the difference actually being of consequence. They agreed Scotland Yard were most likely investigating Carstens' possible involvement in local crimes, and didn't want anyone to hear about it.

- But there might be a way to find out. I'm planning to wire Uncle Arthur when I'm back at the office.

- Uncle Arthur?

- My dear great-uncle, Arthur Conan Doyle. I'm sure he can find out more and will be very interested – unless he's out travelling with his spiritualists.

- So, can't he just ask the spirits?

- There are no dead people involved, so who would he ask? I hope he's in London. And if he is, he's probably already interested. I'll know more tonight.

- Is he really family?

- Yes. And it's probably why I got my job. Bærentzen was duly impressed.

- I can imagine. We've often talked about Sherlock Holmes when he came to ask about new cases.

- And I can confirm that both my parents and I would love to come to your parents' party. They looked absolutely thrilled at the thought. It seems to be quite an honour to be invited.

- It is. Only for the chosen few.

Christian winked at Anna.

- And Helena is coming for tea with my mother in a couple of days. They seem to have a common interest in family planning.

- How?

- My mother hosts meetings about contraception, and as far as I understand, Helena imports various articles that the participants might find interesting. My mother was very quick to ask me to invite her.

- At that lecture?

- Yes. Not that she knew that part of Helena's business at the time – she just guessed at her primary occupation and thought it might be a possibility. Helena confirmed that when we were investigating Leaning-Inger. It should be interesting. My mother encouraged our Marie to join the Copenhagen Maidservant Association, and not just for her own sake. She wants contacts that way because they desperately need more knowledge. I guess she'll also talk to your mother when they meet. The theatre world has the same need, but they probably know more than the maids.

- And luckily for everyone, it's legal. Something the police will do almost anything to keep unchanged.

They reached Hansen's lodgings, where Christian got hold of the landlady and a key, while Anna stayed out of sight.

It looked exactly the same as last time; no one had been inside – not even too clean. The only difference this time was the sunlight, which shone obliquely through the windows, casting long beams of light on the floor. It smelled slightly more of dust and less of cheap cigars.

- I've been through it all – there was nothing to find.

- There must be something somewhere. Everyone has papers, if nothing else about themselves.

Anna took a small hand mirror out of her bag and held it up to the cabinet to see if there was anything behind it. There wasn't. She did the same with the dresser – nothing. The mirror went back into the bag. Then she looked at the chair. It had a worn, padded seat. She pressed it with a couple of fingers up and down the seat, making the fabric creak.

- The sound is different. There's something that sounds like paper. Can the seat be lifted?

Christian tried. It couldn't.

- Turn it upside down.

Christian turned the chair over. It had worn tacks under the seat, which could be pushed aside. There was hessian under the upholstery, which was sewn on three sides but not on the fourth. The holes were there, but the stitches were gone. Anna tried with her fingers to see if there was anything between the layers. There was.

- Got it!

Meanwhile, Christian had been looking at the floor and the light, which made the uneven floorboards cast shadows. There was a shadow under the bed that was different – longer. He got down on his knees and felt with his hands. One floorboard was missing the nails and was a millimetre higher at one end than the other and could be lifted away.

- And here.

Anna waved a passport, which contained a train ticket for the same trip Carstens had taken to Hamburg, and which, for obvious reasons, was unused.

- Looks like he was planning to disappear too. What's under the floor?

- A piece of dirty handkerchief with three diamond rings. Money. German money. Not a fortune – 50 kr. and 10 Reichsmarks. A key to something small that isn't here. A drawing with BB in the corner. Bogense Bank maybe? All interesting and something to pass on to Bugge, but nothing to do with Inger. And then I have to come up with an explanation of why I'm here now and why I didn't find it last time.

- Hmm. Maybe you were sitting at home yesterday and noticed the light coming in through the window and that the floorboards were uneven and got an idea you just had to try out to be certain?

- Exactly. And Madsen is hardly likely to come visit to check which way my windows are facing. Or lift my rug to look at the floorboards...

- Or you could have just talked to me, who explained how to hide things at a boarding school. For example, under floorboards and in loose chair seats. When you want to make sure it's found, of course, if you can think that far ahead.

- How?

- The headmistress usually has a similar boarding school education as do most of the teachers. I doubt there's a single trick left they don't know.

Christian chuckled.

- I'll figure out which explanation fits best when I need it. But it's good to have at least two at the ready... So where did you hide your secrets?

- In my head. The only safe place in a girls' school.

- Assuming you don't talk in your sleep.

Anna looked at him and tilted her head.

- You know what? I've never actually thought about that. Maybe because I've never shared a room with anyone who talked in their sleep. Hmm... Clever you. ... But we better get going. I need to telegraph Uncle Arthur and write a couple of articles first, and I think we've found what we came for.

Anna handed Christian the passport and the ticket, winked at him, and was out of the door on her way back to the office. He got hold of the landlady, who locked up again, and went straight to Bugge while considering his explanation and thinking it was a major loss to the police force, they didn't want to hire detectives with a girls' school education.

Anna found a great story for the newspaper – with a magnificent illustration. Actor Alexander Hogan and sailor Michael McKenna – both long-term inmates at the infamous Folsom penitentiary on the Sacramento River in California, had escaped in the most spectacular manner. The heavily guarded prison with towers and walls was not all that secure.

A construction crane had been erected in the prison yard, which, due to its size, was tethered with a cable to the opposite side of the river – outside the prison. The two inmates who had worked in the prison's workshop had rigged a pulley system, where they could ride at lightning speed, sparks flying, in a homemade sling on a wheel attached to the cable. They were out of prison before the completely bewildered guard on top of one of the towers could even fire warning shots. They were, however, soon recaptured and put back inside.

Afterwards, she telegraphed Windlesham to see if Uncle Arthur was at home. He wasn't. He was at the Metropole Hotel in London. Yes, he had read about the case in the newspaper and was excited to hear that she was writing about it as a journalist, and he would certainly like to attend court to hear more – and inquire with his acquaintances in the police. Naturally.

Fortunately, his brother Innes was on his way to Copenhagen to visit Clara, so Arthur would write as soon as possible and give Innes the letter. Then it was just a matter of waiting, and there was a solo story that would make Bærentzen eat out of her hand.

Bugge was, as always, happy to see his favourite detective, who smilingly handed over the day's findings.

- Just dropped by waiter Hansen's lodgings again. Found a bit under the floorboards.

Bugge took a magnifying glass and held one of the diamond rings under a lamp and whistled.

- C.J.M. – mean anything to you?
- Møinichen!
- Jackpot again, la Cour. How do you do it?

- I get inspired, Bugge. I get inspired. By sunshine and girls' schools.

Christian wriggled his eyebrows and laughed as he sauntered out of the Central Bureau, while Bugge watched him leave.

'He's bloody strange. But it works,' Bugge said to himself as he placed the new evidence in boxes and labelled them with the details.

12.

Innes Conan Doyle dropped by Kronprinsessegade to deliver his brother's letter to Anna, and he also brought some local papers that would normally never reach Copenhagen. In return, he got a hug before hurrying off to Clara, and Anna began reading before sitting down.

It made for a fantastic article that shed new light on the fact that Scotland Yard was indeed conducting investigations, which might be more of a reason for the extradition hassle than the petty squabbling about impossible evidence, and the Copenhagen Detective Office might as well prepare for a definitive refusal very soon.

And dear Uncle Arthur had even had his secretary type the letter with a carbon copy for Christian, who fortunately could read English and – it was rather sweet of Uncle Arthur – with a short, handwritten note directly to the police with an elaborate signature. The original also had a little handwritten personal note to her congratulating her on the job and 'Congratulations to your Editor. He must be very pleased'. He most certainly would.

It was detectives Whitley and Town from Scotland Yard who had turned up on Graven Street by Charing Cross at 8 o'clock on Tuesday morning and arrested Hans Bernhard Carstens at his home. Carstens hadn't come to the door, and they had to knock several times. After some noise, which the detectives interpreted as Carsten attempting to hide something, he opened the door, wearing pyjamas and dressing gown, quite cautiously asking what they wanted. He first claimed to be a Dane with nothing to do with English police – and then claimed to be a British citizen with special rights. They informed him he was arrested at the request of the Danish police in connection with the jewel thefts in Copenhagen.

This stunned Carstens completely, and he kept repeating 'it must be a misunderstanding' while he was getting dressed. He was then handcuffed and taken to the police station. When Whitley was asked if he expected Carstens to be extradited, the answer was a flat no. 'We have a few things to talk to Mr Carstens about first. Such as a burglary at E. J. Needes on Euston Road. The second major jewel theft in London in just a month.' The loot had a value of about £3,000 in jewellery, gold watches, and antiques, and the burglars had entered the shop through a ventilation shaft. They had managed to empty the shop completely, even though the staff were sleeping in an adjacent room. The thieves left through the same shaft, so the sound of the door wouldn't wake anyone. The break-in was only discovered at opening time.

The local newspapers had written about it as being exceptionally bold and skilful. Carstens was of course immediately suspected of this and other burglaries because of the request from Copenhagen. In London, they now believed that both brothers were members of a larger, international gang, and that Hans Bernhard Carstens might be the mastermind behind it. This was also indicated by the correspondence found in Istedgade. The correspondence that the London judge kept saying wasn't incriminating enough for extradition.

Uncle Arthur had allowed himself to remark that it was lucky for Scotland Yard they had been contacted by Copenhagen. Otherwise, they would have been completely in the dark about Euston Road. His personal opinion of the Yard was no better than Sherlock's, as expressed in the books, and he complimented Copenhagen for having detectives who were up to scratch.

As Anna recalled Christian's explanations, that wasn't quite the message they had given the Danish consulate. There was nothing about Bernhard Carstens being suspected of burglaries in London – only the message that the evidence from Copenhagen was inadequate.

There was no doubt that there had been a burglary at E. J. Needes – it was mentioned in the newspapers Innes had brought – but perhaps it was a bit embarrassing for Scotland Yard that they had no idea who the thieves might be until they were contacted by the Copenhagen Detective Office. That would be a tough one to admit. Unless there were things Christian didn't know about, there were quite a few things Scotland Yard hadn't told Copenhagen, even though two burglaries in London had occurred after the contact from Denmark; in fact, the burglary at Needes happened the night before the police showed up at Carstens' flat on Tuesday morning, and there had subsequently been several days to contact Copenhagen about the developments. They could have telegraphed many times. Regardless, it made for a headline of the highest order.

So, this morning, Anna allowed herself to enter the newsroom with a big smile, where, as expected, Bærentzen immediately came out to find out what could bring about such happiness.

- You have a scoop?

he ventured.

- Elementary, my dear Bærentzen.

Anna handed him the letter from Conan Doyle, which he couldn't read beyond recognising the signature and seeing it was addressed to Anna.

- Tell me!

was all he could muster as he sat down, eyes gleaming in anticipation.

Anna explained that both she and the police believed that the delays in extradition were so odd there had to be something behind it, so she got the idea to ask Uncle Arthur if he happened to be in London and would he take a closer look at the case and have a chat with his acquaintances at the Yard? This letter was the result, and yes, they were investigating Bernhard Carstens' more local merits, including planning a major heist in London. She read aloud, translating ad lib.

Bærentzen was ecstatic. A letter directly from Conan Doyle to his newspaper with an article almost written by Conan Doyle himself. It couldn't be better. It was... the only thing that could surpass it would be to meet the man himself, and if it was true that his brother was on the verge of proposing in Copenhagen, it was likely he would pay a visit at the wedding.

Anna was a star, and Bærentzen was the luckiest man alive to have been smart enough to hire her. And she was forgiven the astronomical cost of several telegrams to England and various other countries.

It resulted in a new lunch invitation, and of course, Anna had to stop by the Detective Office to tell them about the content as soon as the article was written. She didn't tell Bærentzen there was a separate copy of the letter just for them.

Anna arrived at the Detective Office with her smile intact, and Christian looked up, understanding as quickly as usual, meaning she only just managed to introduce herself before he was at the counter. This time however, to Christian's surprise, Anna inquired about Madsen, who was in his office, where she was invited in along with Christian and solemnly handed over the copy of the letter from Conan Doyle.

Christian was asked to translate immediately. There was no doubt that it made sense to both Christian and Madsen, who agreed that there would probably soon be a definitive refusal of extradition. They had far too much to ask Carstens back in London for them to let him go. It was deeply frustrating, but understandable.

There was no questioning the accuracy of the content – they were convinced that Conan Doyle had received truthful answers from the two detectives.

Anna smiled kindly at Madsen.

- This is a carbon copy, as you can see – for you from my great uncle, so you can keep it for the case. In return, I hope you'll respect that this is my story, and it's an internal document not to be shared with the rest of the press.

- Your uncle? You're related to Conan Doyle? And yes, of course.

- Yes – through my grandmother. His brother Innes brought the letter to me. He's courting in Copenhagen. Do you have a comment on the extradition case?

- Eh, no, not right now.

- Very well. But I must get back to the newsroom. I have more writing to do today. Gentlemen...

Anna stood up, and both Christian and Madsen hurried to do the same.

- Miss Lendorph.

Christian bowed, and Madsen extended his hand.

- Thank you very much, Miss Lendorph.

Anna left the office, and Christian and Madsen watched her all the way out before sitting down simultaneously and becoming aware of it. They both laughed.

- I assume you're keeping Aftenbladet informed, and that is the reason for this unexpected gesture from the newspaper?

Madsen asked with a half-hearted attempt at an innocent expression.

- Yes, I speak regularly with Miss Lendorph, who excels at sticking to the truth, unlike some others. And who also, incidentally, found the story with the sister and the safe opening competition.

Madsen looked at Christian, whose former fiancée had left him for America, and Miss Lendorph had no ring on, and thought they would make a wonderful couple if it weren't for her job as a journalist. That could cause problems.

- Why isn't Bærentzen on it himself?

- As far as I understand, he was simply unavailable at the time of the break-in at Møinichen's and subsequently also occupied with some family matters, so it was a bit of coincidence. And A... Miss Lendorph is employed to write about foreign affairs, and it looked like an international gang from the start. She had knowledge of a similar burglary in Nice, and she was allowed to continue. I don't think he has regretted it. If he had kept it to himself, there wouldn't have been a letter from Conan Doyle. It's the only local story she's on.

Madsen was reassured. And remembered that Bærentzen had also visited the Detective Office himself recently, as usual, about other things – like the English sailor who had shot himself. If la Cour had managed to impress Miss Lendorph, he didn't need to worry. It was smart of both of them to give him the letter and a nice way to let la Cour shine. There was no doubt that this was what Miss Lendorph had intended. The two of them had something going on; he was sure of it. Just not sure how far it had progressed. Well, it wasn't his business as long as it remained private.

Madsen considered whether to say something, but decided it probably wasn't necessary. La Cour was intelligent, and Miss Lendorph obviously was, too. And women usually stopped working when they got married, and then the problem would solve itself. Until then – and if – there were probably limits to how much they could see each other and what they could talk about.

- You went to waiter Hansen's lodgings again, Bugge says – and found the diamond rings with Møinichen's stamp under a floorboard? What prompted you to do that?

Christian was prepared, and today's meeting had made it much easier.

- I told Miss Lendorph about the case, and mentioned that there was nothing of interest at his lodgings, and she asked if I had looked under the floorboards. I thought it was a joke at first, but she explained it was one of the preferred hiding spots at boarding schools, and that it was odd there was nothing; he must have personal papers like everyone else. So, I decided to go and look. And the sunlight was shining exactly at the right angle to make a board under the bed cast a shadow, and it could be lifted.

- So, Miss Lendorph has also made a valuable contribution? I admit, Bærentzen has given comments in the past that have led us further. By the way, I must pass on thanks from Haack for securing the connection to the Møinichen burglary. Well done, la Cour.

Madsen stood up to indicate that the meeting was over, and Christian went back to his desk.

Interesting morning. Right now, he had to wait for Haack's interrogation in the jewel case, but there was still the murder of Leaning-Inger. Who murdered Inger – and why? At least he could enjoy the fact that the women in his life seemed to be good friends. Intelligent, resourceful, opportunistic... Christian was impressed by the way Anna had introduced herself to Madsen, but it was a brilliant move. Madsen was happy, and if anyone from the Detective Office saw him with Anna, there was a reason – and he had Madsen's indirect approval, despite her being a journalist. Good thing he had emphasised the international aspect. There was no doubt that Madsen now saw Anna as a bit more than 'just a journalist'.

Christian was just as good at reading faces as Madsen – and pauses – and a conclusion had clearly been reached and a decision made to accept. But also, an unspoken warning to be careful not to mix things too much. He couldn't help but smile at the thought of Anna and Helena as detectives. If Madsen only knew.

Funny how the family connection with Conan Doyle somehow legitimised Anna's interest in both crime and journalism even though she was a woman. It was a bit more acceptable, good common sense to use it.

He thought of Helena and her import business of 'personal items' from France. He had helped her occasionally with the correspondence. It might become easier now that she was collaborating with a doctor who was also fluent in French. Perhaps she would end up as a very wealthy businesswoman in a Copenhagen with fewer unwanted children. She certainly deserved it, and so did Copenhagen.

Christian decided to ask Anna as soon as possible about what else was on the curriculum at girls' schools in Europe because it seemed there was more to learn. Anna had started fencing and shooting with both pistol and longbow at the boarding school in Switzerland, so what sports did they have at other places?

And then there was their 'extra curriculum', as she called it. All the things one could learn if you knew the right people – beyond the established one. There were always at least two, she had explained. The official one with the exams and then at least one other that you were initiated into – sometimes even one more, that handed you rather tough survival lessons. Afterwards, you were ready for all the challenges society had to offer – the known rules, the unwritten rules, and what to do when rules were suspended – often in diplomatic contexts – and how to send out that 'rules don't apply to me' signal, which Anna herself had perfected.

And apparently, there was also a repertoire of more practical skills. At least it sounded like you didn't come home from Switzerland or England without being able to pick a lock. Other skills were only hinted at.

He looked forward to learning more at some point – preferably a whole course. Not that he hadn't picked up a thing or two from his colleagues and 'customers' at Nørrebro, but it sounded like the boarding school girls were rather more skilled.

Lunch with Bærentzen turned out to be the expected interrogation about Conan Doyle, and it was clear he was keen to know if there was a wedding on the horizon in Copenhagen, where one might be lucky enough to meet the famous author. Anna could confirm that at least that was what Innes wanted, but the engagement hadn't yet been declared. The expectation, however, was that the wedding would take place at Holmen's Kirke, which was the Swendsen family's parish church.

They also touched on the latest publication – 'Sherlock Holmes' New Adventures', which Anna had to admit she found rather dull.

- I'm no longer impressed by Sherlock's detective work. I've seen better in Copenhagen,

she explained to Bærentzen, who nodded.

- La Cour?

Yes. He's considerably more thorough. And there are things Holmes doesn't even notice. And why ask someone to get their thoughts in order before they explain, when the way they explain reveals more when they haven't? It's all so contrived, so self-satisfied; the first story actually has no resolution, and there's some voodoo completely unrelated to the rest. Nonsense...

- The journalist's curse,

Bærentzen chuckled.

- Fiction easily becomes boring when reality is so much more interesting.

Anna agreed. Which author would have come up with Romeo and Julio and the rest of the 'opera cast', as Christian called the several-page-long list of crooks from Sweden? Or the safe-opening competition in Chicago?

- You're right. But at least the Sherlock Holmes stories are fun on film.

- And Olsen makes the best ones, no doubt about it. Even the English love them.

- Viggo Larsen is a very good Sherlock.

Afterwards, Anna tried to find out more about waiter Hansen, and it turned out he was the son of a former brewer in Odder and the youngest of seven sons. The father had died, and the mother had gone to America with five of the sons. Only Frederik and one brother, who was a skilled pharmacist, had stayed in Denmark, and both now lived in Copenhagen. She wondered why Frederik had become a burglar instead of going to America. It wasn't a story worth writing, and she pitied the brother, who was probably very relieved to have a name as common as Hansen right now.

Back home, Anna had tea with her mother, who had had Helena visiting in the morning and was thrilled. She talked about Helena's import business, and they had discussed products, qualities, and prices, and Agnes had suggested a couple of manufacturers in Germany who could deliver better quality at lower prices.

They had agreed something had to be done about the maids, so Agnes would have a talk with Marie about how the association worked. Whether it was possible, for example, to hold meetings on family planning within the association.

Agnes and Helena had already made a deal for Helena to be the sole supplier to Agnes's clinic, and Helena could refer to Agnes as well.

- And I think Ida has a network in the theatres where it would also be relevant. I'll ask at the party.

There was no doubt that Agnes was looking forward to the upcoming party at la Cour's, and so was Anna.

- Maybe we should think about costumes – it's not long?

Anna suggested.

- You'd make a beautiful Columbine.

- We could also dress up together – Zeus, Hera, and Athena, for example?

- Let's ask your father what he thinks. He probably has an idea, too.

Anna remembered Helena might come as Helen of Troy, so maybe they should leave the Greek theme to her? She could easily compete with her namesake if she wanted to.

- Columbine sounds reasonable. Who can sew?

- Maybe you should ask Christian. His mother must know the best.

- Good idea.

Christian did his exercises as usual when he got home, but it was Leaning-Inger who was at the forefront of his mind. Was she the one who had visited Hansen, and if so – why? And if not – who had visited her and possibly killed her? Were there others besides Hansen who wore diamond rings?

He went to dinner with his parents. He told his them that everyone had accepted the invitation to the party and was very much looking forward to it.

- Have you thought about a costume? Harlequin, perhaps?

- Hmm. Sounds like a good idea. Will Nina be sewing?

- If I ask her, and I will.

Nina was Ida's favourite theatre seamstress, and if she made a Harlequin costume for Christian, he would be the handsomest Harlequin Copenhagen had ever seen. It fitted nicely with Ida's plans. She and her husband would be Tyroleans and perform a yodelling act together. She knew she looked good in a dirndl, and Erik still had the legs for lederhosen. It also provided a good excuse to serve beer at the party. Something she knew many of the younger guests preferred when they got hot from all the dancing.

Later in the evening, Christian once again made the rounds of Inger's favourite places and ended up at Schooner-Larsen's, where he eventually found Olga, who had been closer to Inger than most. Maybe Inger had said something?

Christian sat down with Olga, who looked up expectantly and immediately put her expectations on hold when she saw who it was.

- Oh, it's you.

- Sorry, Olga. But there's a little something for your memory, if you can help.

Olga made a big show of looking attentive.

- What do you want to know?

- Did you talk to Leaning-Inger before she died?

- When was that?

- In the last couple of weeks. Did she meet a new man, have new plans?

Olga got a brandy and held out the glass again. A nod from Christian got it refilled.

- Inger always met new men. Those who knew her ran as soon as they saw her coming round the corner.

Olga laughed and held out the glass again. And got it refilled.

- But there was one she talked about, now that you mention it. A waiter, I think. With a diamond ring. She kept waffling on about that diamond ring. I don't think she'd ever seen one up close before. Maybe she thought he was loaded and wanted to swap the sailor.

Olga's attention drifted off, and Christian made sure she got another brandy. There was no immediate danger of it affecting Olga's memory. That would take a lot more.

- Did she say anything about him?

- Not really. But I think she had plans. She wanted something.

- To visit him?

- Maybe. She did ask about the price of a tram ticket. But she never said much.

Olga looked blank again. There would probably be no more revelations, because, as Olga herself said, Inger was rarely forthcoming with details. That Olga could remember anything at all was a small miracle, but perhaps the diamond ring had made the difference. It wasn't a topic they usually had occasion to talk about.

Christian thanked Olga, made sure she got another refill and put a two-crown coin by the glass.

- Thanks, Olga. Get yourself something to eat.

He greeted a couple of other acquaintances and asked about Osvaldo, who still hadn't shown up, and about Inger's sailor boyfriend Peter, whom no one had seen for just as long and who also risked being beaten up and delivered to the nearest police station as soon as he showed his face. They didn't normally meddle in each other's businesses, but murder was different.

Christian walked back home through the quiet night, where the moon reflected in the water of Peblingesøen. He enjoyed walking through the quiet streets, when the city noise was replaced by light steps that usually stopped at a safe distance from his imposing figure. Only one person had once been drunk enough to accost him and had, very quickly, but too late, regretted doing so.

That Inger had visited Hansen wasn't so mysterious if she thought he had money. That he had visited Inger, however – that was very odd. That he knew where she lived was definitely mysterious. Christian went through many scenarios in his head before he reached his room and went to bed, dreaming that Inger chopped off one of Hansen's fingers. The one with the diamond ring, of course.

Christian woke up with a start from his dream. Could that be the reason? Had Inger stolen something from Hansen, which he came to find? She was a skilled pickpocket when she wasn't too drunk. Maybe there were more floorboards in need of lifting. He decided to go back to Inger's lodgings again – with a powerful torch.

The note from the Royal Danish Embassy in London prompted more swearing than had ever been heard in Madsen's office.

- I have the honour to report that Hans Bernhard Carstens, according to a note from the British Foreign Office, was released today as the magistrate did not find the evidence submitted sufficient to justify his detention pending extradition,

Madsen read aloud from the letter.

Madsen and Christian looked at each other and at Commissioner Eugen Petersen, who had arrived and was as likely to self combust as was Madsen.

- Are they complete idiots in England? They have him, they have a case themselves, they rushed the arrest through because they considered him capable of escaping without a trace, and then they release him??

- It will probably be worse for themselves. There is no sign that he intends to end his career, and he can't go to the continent without being apprehended.

- They're insane. Utterly mad. Besides being stupid, rude, hopeless amateurs. No wonder Conan Doyle mocks Scotland Yard. There's apparently a very good reason for it. At least we have the other two.

The Commissioner looked despairingly at Madsen and then at Christian.

- Your work is exemplary, la Cour. Please continue along that line. He nodded to Christian as a sign that he could leave. Madsen looked at the Commissioner:

- Is there anything we can do?

Petersen shook his head.

- Nothing at all. The Ministry of Foreign Affairs can express their dissatisfaction and encourage updating the old treaty. That's it.

- And then we can sit and wait for new articles about jewel thefts in England?

- I'm certain Miss Lendorph will keep us informed. On the front page.

Madsen chuckled wryly.

- Speaking of which. How's the matter of 'women in the police' progressing?

- Slowly. We still receive inquiries from associations, including the Danish Women's Society, both for and against, and have asked the police in Los Angeles about their several years of experience, and they are very positive. Chicago as well. And Stockholm. And Finland. Mainz. Munich. Kristiania is in the process of hiring two. Politically, however, there isn't much enthusiasm in this city, so it could take years. Shame. We are hopelessly behind on that front.

Anna received a reply from Jeanne in Paris, who had been to Rue de la Paix and visited Saumenbluhm, who had a very prestigious establishment. There was no spider jewellery of any kind; however, the selection of rings with emeralds and diamonds was large – all his own brand. Some rings matched the description, but they were not unusual, so there was nothing that could be used as evidence. Jeanne promised to keep an eye out in case spider jewellery appeared elsewhere, but it wasn't a sought-after motif in Paris. Jeanne also sent a newspaper clipping from a local Parisian newspaper, which she thought would amuse Anna. It did – and also quickly found its way into the paper as today's entertainment:

Scenic Landscape on Jupiter.

Abroad, many famous people, scientists, and authors experiment with spiritualism. The recently deceased French poet Victorien Sardou was a spiritualist, and in a trance, he drew this picture, which is supposed to depict a scenic landscape on Jupiter.

Jupiter was apparently inhabited by winged creatures and others with a penchant for acrobatics. But that wasn't quite enough. Anna found another story – this time from the USA – which had it all: love, money, and a Copenhagen protagonist:

An eccentric, who had wandered across America, educated at the University of Copenhagen and now a millionaire, had just married a maid, whom he had met at a meeting where he had lectured on socialism. It was these lectures – and his vagabond lifestyle – that had made him a millionaire. However, marriage meant that he would now stop wandering around as a preacher of socialism and settle in Duluth and trade in copper stocks. A story with a certain irony, Anna thought.

13.

Christian went back to Inger's room – this time alone and carrying the most powerful torch he could find. He nodded at the few residents he met on the way and went straight up. The stench still lingered in the timber and the musty newspapers, but it had mixed so much with the other odours that one would have to be particularly attentive to notice.

He put his bag down, put on gloves, and entered the room where Inger had been found to see if there was anything he hadn't noticed before – there wasn't. The bloodstains were still there – and the dirt on the floor. Apparently, no one had been around since she was found. He went back to Inger and Peter's room. Here, however, someone had visited since he was last there.

There were footprints that hadn't been there before. The mattress had been lifted and not put back right. It had been cut into, making the straw spill out, and rats had moved in. Christian grabbed it, causing squeaks, and a rat fell out and ran past him and through a knothole at floor level next to him. There was otherwise nothing in the mattress but old straw and rat droppings, as far as he could see.

The bed frame had been moved out and back in again, leaving traces in the dirt. The two plates, tin cups, spoons, and knives had been moved around, and when he shone the light under the table, he could see someone had had a feel around. The table's only drawer only had a fire steel, a couple of matches, and a small sooty rag in it. Christian tried to remember how it had looked last time. There had been a dishcloth hanging on the wall, which was now gone, and there had been a string with a waxed cloth bag out of the window, like at all the other windows. That was gone, too.

Christian focused on the floorboards, shining the flashlight diagonally in a tight pattern. It was hard to see if there were loose boards, as they were roughly hewn and not flat. There were also missing nails – maybe they had been sold? Christian gathered his coat around his legs so it wouldn't touch the floor and squatted down, looking around carefully turning on his heels. Perhaps a board under the bed?

He tried if a board could be lifted. It could. He shone the light down into the hole. It was empty. There was only a thick layer of dust at the bottom, and it was clear something had been there, and that someone had put their hands down – there were marks of what must have been paper and of fingers and at one end of something that had left a round impression in the dust. Christian went out for the bag so he could try to for fingerprints on the underside of the table and make a plaster cast of the marks in the hole under the floorboards. The results went into the bag. Christian put the board back and went out. He put the string back on the door, took off the gloves, and put them in a paper bag. They were now so dirty he didn't want them touching anything else.

Then he walked back to the office with a stop at the telephone kiosk at Dronning Louise's Bridge, where he called Anna and asked to meet in the afternoon. He could have taken a tram, but he enjoyed walking while trying to collect his thoughts.

Someone had been there, and someone had emptied the secret place. The question was whether it was the same person. If Hansen had searched for something, he would hardly have removed a dirty dishcloth and a food bag. Did he discover the hiding place, or had Peter been round emptying the room? Had he found something that made him kill Inger? The mystery hadn't exactly become smaller, but at least he knew more. Someone had been there after Inger died, and after he had been there with Strømmen.

The harbour master had already been informed that if anyone saw Peter, he should be arrested, so there wasn't much else he could do – on the other hand, he had to tell assessor Haack, who was questioning Hansen, that there was more to ask about than anyone could have guessed. The question was how.

It was Anna and Helena who had found out that Hansen had probably visited Inger, and it was on a Sunday trip he and Anna had found out that Inger might have visited Hansen. But he didn't need explain that Anna's and Helena's detective excursion was his idea. Anna was a journalist after all and had, entirely on her own initiative, received news from London. So, naturally, it was her idea, and Anna – with her uncle – he smiled to himself, had collaborated with the police, so maybe he should just stop worrying and ask Haack to question Hansen about Leaning-Inger. Haack didn't need to give Hansen any reason.

He decided to contact Haack right away and, among other things, find out when the next interrogation would be so he could be there himself. But first, he had to stop by Bugge with fingerprints and a plaster cast. Perhaps Bugge knew what could have made the marks in the dust.

Bugge examined the fingerprints.

- They're no good,

he said, then looked at the plaster cast, holding it up to the light and turning it around.

- Paper – several sheets, quite stiff. Some fabric – maybe a handkerchief. And something round I wouldn't dare to guess at. Where did you find this?

- Under a floorboard at Leaning-Inger's.

- You've been there again – why?

Christian explained about his dream and his suspicion that Inger was somehow involved in the jewel theft, about Anna's trip to Inger's room – minus Helena – which he explained as her own idea, and about the visit from an unknown man who sounded like Hansen. And if there was something under one board, there could be more loose floorboards.

- Bugge found Christian's explanation plausible enough, except for one rather significant detail.

- Miss Lendorph went out there, discovered something, told you, and didn't write a sentence about it in the paper?

Bugge eyed Christian, who had to think quickly.

- Anna says she doesn't want to write guesswork – there is quite enough of that. And it might warn someone who should be caught. And it's still only her – and now us – who knows until Haack maybe gets Hansen to talk, so there's something to write about that's credible. I'll talk to Haack later today.

- Anna – I see. But of course, you've probably had to meet up a few times. And having a good relationship with the press never hurts.

Bugge was about to burst out laughing at Christian, who didn't quite know what to say, and who he was sure either had an affair with Miss Lendorph or at the very least hoped to start one. He decided to be nice to Christian.

- She's been able to talk to the women better than the police. Usually, you can't get a word out of them. They just glare at you, if they haven't just disappeared altogether. It'll be interesting to hear what Haack can make of that information.

- Exactly. ... Do you have a photograph of Inger?

Bugge found Inger's file, which contained only a few descriptions, fingerprints, and photos. One of them was taken just before the funeral, when Inger was washed, combed, made up and laid out, taken from the side she had been lying on, where the rats hadn't gnawed at her face. He handed the picture to Christian.

- What do you need that for?

- Take to Hansen's colleagues and see if they've seen her. You never know.

Bugge watched Christian leave, thinking like Madsen that Christian's collaboration with Miss Lendorph was somewhat unorthodox and probably much closer than he let on. But if she could know something this interesting and not write it in the paper – which meant she hadn't told Bærentzen – then this Miss Lendorph was quite extraordinary and currently not a threat to police work. Rather, the contrary.

He hadn't for a moment thought that Leaning-Inger could have anything to do with the jewel case, but maybe she did, albeit only peripherally. Well, la Cour – and Miss Lendorph – were apparently on the case, so there would be more to come. It was just a matter of waiting. Bugge smiled expectantly to himself.

On his way back to the office, Christian stopped by the post office and picked up the last cream-coloured envelope of the season.

Anna had just hung the rapier back on the wall when Christian arrived. She made sure to ask about a seamstress right away – in fact; he hadn't even had time to take his coat off.

- Nina. My mother always uses Nina. She's very good. I don't actually know her last name. Should I call my mother? There's not much time.

He took his coat off, and they went into the parlour, where Agnes was talking to Marie.

- Christian needs to borrow the phone if you want the best seamstress for your costume.

- Yes, please. Of course. It's right there.

Agnes looked excited; Marie hurried out, and Christian got hold of his mother, who – how lucky could one be – had Nina visiting to fit her dirndl and could thus come to the phone herself.

- Nina is with my mother – wouldn't you rather speak with her yourself, Dr Lendorph?

Agnes nodded and took the receiver, making an appointment with Nina, who, of course, was happy to help any guest at the la Cour party. Anna and Christian went back to Anna's room, where Christian asked about the costume she had chosen.

- My mother suggested Columbine.

- Good choice. No cumbersome props, reasonably comfortable and not too hot.

He paused for effect, looking at Anna, who didn't quite know what to make of the answer until she noticed the twinkle in his eyes.

- And of course, you'll look stunning as Columbine.

- What about you? What will you be?

- Haven't quite decided yet,

he lied, knowing full well there was one option only: Harlequin. He wondered if he should take the choice of Columbine as a sign from the gods or from Anna's mother. Probably the latter.

Marie brought tea and sandwiches and looked rather disappointed finding Anna at the desk and Christian in the armchair without even a hint of hanky-panky in the air, so she put the tray on the table, said 'there you go', and left again.

Christian explained the atmosphere at the office when the final rejection had come from London.

- I've never heard Madsen swear like that before. Or express himself so undiplomatically about anyone. Or Petersen, for that matter. There was almost smoke coming out of their ears. They were very much in agreement with Uncle Arthur regarding Scotland Yard's lack of competence.

- It'll probably be worst for the Yard.

- That was our conclusion as well. But we can't do anything.

They ate the sandwiches and drank the tea.

- But there's something else. I went by Inger's today – I dreamt about her and Hansen last night – that she chopped a finger off him. I woke up with the thought that she might have stolen from him, and that's why he had come by. And maybe she also had loose floor-boards.

- Did she?

- She did. And something had been hidden there, but it had gone, leaving only an imprint in the dust. It was also clear someone had been there after she died, but it could just as well be her sailor boyfriend. A dishcloth and the food bag hanging from the window were missing, and I can't imagine Hansen taking it.

- He might have thought she hid something in the food bag? And maybe used the dishcloth for some-thing? Wrapped something in it?

- Strømmen looked in the food bag when we were there. It was empty, but we left it. I went to Bugge with fingerprints and a plaster cast from the floor. The fingerprints were useless, but he confirmed that there had been sheets of paper and maybe something in a handkerchief under the floor. I got a photo of Inger too.

- Can I have a look?

Christian handed Anna the picture.

- So, she looked like this when she was alive?

- Not really. I don't think I've ever seen her that neat. I'll have to go back to the pavilion again to ask if it was her visiting, and if Hansen said anything about someone stealing from him.

- Did Inger steal?

- She was a skilled pickpocket, if she wasn't too drunk.

- So, she could have taken something from Hansen, maybe something valuable, and perhaps showed up to blackmail him, and he came to find what she had stolen? And killed her?

- Maybe. For now, it's just speculation. But I've talked to assessor Haack, who'll be interrogating Hansen again tomorrow. It'll be interesting to hear what he has to say. Inger hasn't been mentioned at all so far.

- What did you tell Haack?

- That you've been doing some journalistic research, talked to the ladies, and found out that Hansen might have been there. You've already demonstrated your journalistic talents admirably, so it didn't come as a surprise. Madsen's been around boasting about the letter from Uncle Arthur.

- Very practical letter. I'm writing to him to explain that it was received with enthusiasm both at the newsroom and the Detective Office. Bærentsen was almost beside himself, so I let him keep the original. He would have framed it if not a bit embarrassing. Maybe he'll do it at home.

- You can certainly pass on greetings from both Madsen and the Commissioner and thank him for his trust in the Danish police. His praise was duly noted, and the letter was translated and shown to Bugge and all the top brass in the police and the Ministry of Justice, and to Jørgensen. Probably the king too.

- Who's Jørgensen?

- He was my superior at Nørrebro – and my teacher at the Police Association's courses. The detective bag is his invention; he's writing a textbook – a Danish version of Gross – and working on coding fingerprints so they can be telegraphed. He was a fantastic boss. It was he who suggested I should be a detective. Christian looked up, and a shelf on the bookcase caught his eye.

- You've got new books – they're arranged different-ly. Christian got up and inspected the bookcase, gaping.

- You've bought Gross' textbook? The big German edition. There's also a Danish one, you know.

- I thought it could be useful. It's certainly interesting, although not suitable for bedtime reading. A bit too heavy, and you get bruises if you fall asleep on it.

Christian chuckled.

- I know. I've tried – the bruises too. Have you read it all?

- No. Just reached the chapter on Gaunersprache. A fascinating mix of languages. The most amazing piece of cultural history. It should be a university subject.

- Or extra curriculum at girls' schools?

Anne laughed.

- Not necessary, but an interesting idea.

The staff at the Esplanade Pavilion greeted Christian warmly and didn't seem to recall his presence there on Sunday with Anna. He showed them the picture of Inger and asked if she had been around to speak to Hansen. One of them confirmed that she could have been, but the woman had been dirty and drunk, so he wouldn't swear it was the same person. But there was a definite resemblance.

Christian also inquired if Hansen had mentioned being robbed, but they didn't think so, and they didn't really talk to him much. About him, yes – with him, no. Only work-related stuff, nothing else. He didn't invite confidence – he was too arrogant and kept himself to himself. They had been very surprised by the woman's visit, which they had found extremely amusing. She wasn't exactly a refined acquaintance. Understandable he wanted her gone and had tried to drag her out of the restaurant by force, which was necessary, by the look of it.

Christian tried to make sense of it all on the way back. Inger and Hansen must have met each other at a pub or on the street, where Inger had emptied his pockets of something valuable, which she might have intended to either sell back to him – maybe one of the rings – or use for blackmail. And then he had sought her out to get it back. At least that made sense. But it would have been more like Inger to have it with her at the pavilion, so he could have just taken it from her, couldn't he?

Maybe they never got that far. Perhaps he just panicked and wanted her out, and she never got a chance to say anything. But how would he know her address? Was it a coincidence – or was it someone else entirely who had passed by the third backyard, or – perhaps also a possibility – had Jeppe just made something up to get some money and had heard about waiter Hansen and his diamond rings from the gossip, which surely had circulated there as everywhere else? Even among those who couldn't read a paper themselves. Maybe he should find Jeppe and have a little chat. If it was just something he had made up, it was important to remove it from the equation.

During today's interrogation of waiter Hansen, Haack showed him the photograph of Inger and asked him to explain their acquaintance. Hansen looked completely thrown but refused to say anything beyond 'don't know her', which was a blatant lie. Once again, he was not forthcoming, and little brother Carstens had nothing to add either. More was needed if anything was to be extracted from those two.

Haack looked at Christian, who understood his unspoken plead. His work was not yet finished. But first, there was just the small matter of the last ball of the season.

14.

Christian arrived as punctual usual and was greeted by the countess of Chambord, who, also as usual, sparkled. He received his dance card and his fee and glanced at the card. There were no newcomers, which would also have been unusual for the last ball.

The orchestra struck up, and the dance began, but the evening unfolded... not as usual. First, Christian had decided – again – to hold back on the champagne, and second, he had by now memorised all the jewellery not only from Copenhagen but also from the other major robberies in Europe, where Anna had provided him with photos or descriptions. Something caught his attention. And not just jewels.

During a brief intermission, while politely conversing a duchess, he caught sight of the countess engrossed in conversation with a dark-haired man in his thirties. The light sparkled from the countess's jewels, and suddenly her tiara looked familiar to him. It closely resembled the tiara from Nice. And the man... what was it about that man? He attempted to respond politely to the duchess's remarks on the heat and the light, while rifling through his memory and the 'opera cast' from Sweden. The Count of Pierini. But he had let his gaze linger on the couple for a moment too long; the countess noticed his attention and said something to the count, who immediately disappeared.

The music started up again, and Christian danced on – gliding across the floor with one fortunate lady after another, all wearing blissful smiles and sighing with delight.

As the ball ended, the countess came over with a glass of champagne, which she handed to Christian, and then took another from a tray held by a waiter.

- A final toast after the last dance. I presume I can count on you for next season?

- Of course.

Christian drank the champagne and went to find his coat and hat.

Much later, when he woke up with a blinding headache, he found himself tied to a bed in a place he didn't recognise. His moustache and Russian order were gone – evidently, someone knew they were props, and as far as he knew, the countess was the only one who could have guessed. So, she had to be involved.

'Idiot', he thought to himself. 'Of course, she is – she was the one who handed you a glass of champagne, which must have been spiked with something knocking you out after just a couple of minutes.'

He was still wearing his evening dress and patent leather shoes, and someone had even given him a thin blanket for cover.

Christian tried to listen for clues as to his location. There was a faint sound of traffic from a tiny, high-set window – the room resembled servants' quarters at the top of a mansion. It could be in the countess's own house. He sniffed. Lime, damp wood, brick, mould, dust... It smelled of rain and rooms unoccupied for a long time, and it was freezing. So probably high under the roof. He looked around.

He was lying on a a thin mattress on a narrow iron bed; there was a chest of drawers, a washstand, a small table, a battered trunk, and nothing else. The walls were papered with yellowing, damp-stained wallpaper with small bouquets of flowers. Maid's room, he concluded. Unused maid's room. There was no sound of people nearby.

The effort made him fall asleep again, and when he woke up for the second time, the ropes had been replaced with handcuffs, chaining one arm to a bedpost leaving the other hand free; the small table had been placed beside the bed with some food and water and – how considerate – a chamber pot put on the floor next to it. They had even made it possible for him to use it. He ate the food, drank the water, and used the chamber pot. If only he could use his head as well, he thought, but it felt switched off. He just managed thinking that the food was a good sign – surely, they wouldn't feed someone they intended to kill – and they could have done that right away instead of bothering to drag him up here. He was probably just being sidelined for a while, and it might have been improvised because he had looked at the countess's jewellery for just a bit too long. He felt drowsy again – they'd probably put something into the food as well; he barely realised before falling asleep again.

At the Detective Office, they were beginning to worry about the absence of la Cour, who was normally very punctual. Madsen was concerned. The jewel case had loose ends; one Carstens had been released and could have come back in disguise and under a false name, and they could have all sorts of associates that no one knew about, and who would like to ensure la Cour didn't get in the way any more than he already had. He was highly skilled, and that usually made enemies.

Madsen called Christian's landlady, who hadn't seen him at breakfast, and who was therefore also very concerned. If he didn't attend because of work, he always told her, she explained. She let herself into his room and then informed Madsen that everything was tidy; the bed was made; he hadn't been home since the day before, and no one else had been there. It looked like he had just left, as far as she could tell.

Madsen then called Miss Lendorph, hoping she might know something – perhaps he had been there? It was somewhat inappropriate, but he could refer to the jewel case, so he had an excuse. But she hadn't heard from him either and was also rather puzzled. Madsen explained his landlady hadn't seen him at breakfast and even provided his address, which Anna didn't know, except that it was on Vestergade. She wondered if it should be seen as an invitation to do a bit of private investigation. The police didn't yet have enough reason to treat him as missing.

Anna was mystified. Christian had – as far as she knew – told her everything about his investigations in the jewel case – and everything about Leaning-Inger – so if he had been somewhere in connection with either case, she should have known. But there had been some quiet days while everyone had been wondering how to proceed when neither Hansen nor Carstens would talk, and they hadn't seen each other, as there was nothing new. Anna had attended to her work, her fencing, and her shooting, and both had had visits from Nina to have their costumes fitted for the party, which was only a week away now.

It was time to think like a detective, so Anna decided to visit Christian's lodgings, and since it sounded like his landlady didn't care for female visitors, she would wait until nighttime and make use of some of the extra skills she had acquired at school. She arrived at Christian's boarding-house at midnight, dressed in dark grey clothing and armed with her Schouboe and a set of special tools, custom-made by a watchmaker in Lausanne who made a good profit from 'school sets,' and who had micro-engraved them just in case. Anna knew this because she had expected it, looked for the marks, and carefully removed them.

It was a simple matter to pick the lock, but it wasn't quite as easy to find Christian's room since there were no names on the doors. She had to sniff her way around. Only at one door was there a faint smell of Penhaligon's

Hammam Bouquet on the handle. She picked the lock and entered, closing the door behind her, and turning on the light.

Christian's room was spacious. There was a wash-stand, a valet, a giant mirror almost floor-to-ceiling with a mahogany frame, a large wardrobe with mirrors in the doors on the opposite wall, and a bed protruding from the wall in between. There was a writing desk, a table with two chairs, a padded armchair, and an etagere with souvenirs from his ballet days, including a large framed photo of himself surrounded by other dancers, and several smaller photos; mostly of Christian on stage. There was a large framed photo, identical to the one he had in his wallet.

It was obvious he hadn't been home last night. The bed was neatly made; everything was tidy, and his usual clothes were hanging where they should be. There was a large open jewellery box in red leather on the table, which seemed to have contained something to wear around the neck. On the table was also an invitation on thick cream-coloured paper with an envelope next to it, addressed to – Anna gasped and had to read it twice – Chretien, Conte de Namours, with a post office box address in Copenhagen. There were several more of them in a silver rack on the writing desk. All invitations to balls. The latest one to a ball last night.

Anna looked in the wardrobe, which should have contained evening dress or something similar – it didn't. No dress shoes either, but instead two pairs of Oxfords that he used for daily wear along with the suits she had seen, and a hanger with ties that matched perfectly in colours, a black bow tie, but no white one – and the Harlequin costume, Nina had told her about.

She smiled at the costume. And remembered the invitations to balls, where he apparently hadn't come back from the last one. So, he had gone to the ball, appropriately dressed, and with something around his neck, which, judging from the box, could be an order of some kind, and had not come home. No need to search for more here.

She wasn't surprised he hadn't said anything – it could be a very long explanation, which, incidentally, was none of her business since they had nothing going on but the solving of the jewel thefts and Inger, but...

Anna took the latest invitation and put it in her coat pocket, turned off the light, and quietly locked the door behind her. She tiptoed out and just as gently locked the front door, hoping no one had heard anything. It didn't seem so, so she disappeared down the stairs and out onto the street. She had her Schouboe in one sleeve – no taking chances. There was no need. Copenhagen had a quiet night. Perhaps because it had started to drizzle.

Anna was cold and wet and worried when she reached home, but at least she had an idea how he had disappeared and – if she was lucky – where he might still be. The question was more whether he was alive – or had fled. Who was the countess of Chambord? She felt she had seen the name before – perhaps in some society column? She was apparently the organiser of balls for the upper classes, and Christian had been invited under a false name and with a false title of count. Perhaps she was just as fake? It was certainly a fantastic cover if you wanted to deal in stolen jewels.

There was no doubt that tomorrow would mean a trip to Bredgade with undivided interest in door signs and facade architecture. And a look in the Blue Book on peerage, which was on the desk – and if that wasn't enough – a telegram to Paris. She dared not think more about what Christian was doing under a false name in that company right now.

Next morning at the office, a thorough reading of the Blue Book revealed that there were no counts of Namours or countesses of Chambord in Denmark, so Anna sent a telegram to Jeanne in Paris, asking her to investigate the matter and wire back – Anna would cover the costs, and it was urgent. She then took a walk down Bredgade, where it was obvious that mansion owners didn't think it necessary to have nameplates, and they all had locked gates, and – she assumed – someone to keep an eye on them. She made sure not to look too curious.

Anna returned to the office to write her usual stories and had to pull herself together to gather her thoughts into something remotely coherent.

Finally, there was a reply from Jeanne, informing her that there had been no counts of Chambord since 1884 and no countesses since 1886, and there had never been anyone named de Namours. There had been dukes of Nemours with an 'e' – not an 'a' – but not anymore and no counts. Both titles were false.

Anna could easily imagine a fake countess as a major trading hub of stolen jewellery – but Christian? There had to be something else. The question was what? And the question was not least whether she should inform Madsen. She could claim his hostess had let her in. But would it help Christian or just make his situation even more dangerous, if he... Anna found it difficult to think 'is not already dead'? Inger was dead, and she couldn't have posed any real danger to anyone. Christian, on the other hand, could.

She decided she would wait until tomorrow to talk to Madsen, and that she had to find out what was in the mansion – and if Christian miraculously still happened to be there. He could have been assaulted on the street, he could have been killed and taken away long ago, or – almost worse – he could have disappeared of his own accord with his share of the loot and a new identity as a French count. He would have no trouble looking the part.

She had to get hold of Helena, who could reach a network she couldn't get near and who might have seen Christian if he had left the mansion. Fortunately, Helena had a telephone – and she was at home. Anna simply explained that Christian had disappeared, his boss didn't know where he was, and he had left his room the night before yesterday wearing evening dress. Would she send out a message to look for him?

Helena got worried and immediately promised that absolutely everyone would look out for him.

Anna assumed Madsen had probably informed his parents. She thought of his mother, who must be sick with worry. She handed in her articles before deadline, grateful that neither Rasmussen nor Bærentzen had shown up, and went home and tried to read Gross while waiting for it to get dark so she could take a closer look at the mansion – if possible, from the inside. Her parents were going out to dinner, so she asked Marie for some cold supper, which made Marie very happy, as she could then go to the cinema with a friend.

Anna didn't get much reading done. The letters danced before her eyes, which to her surprise, filled with tears. She wasn't usually one to cry. She pictured the image of Ida and little Christian dancing and looked at the invitation from the countess. Perhaps that was the connection? Maybe it was about dancing? Acting? He had said he loved it with a warmth and longing in his voice she hadn't heard before when they sat at the Esplanade Pavilion.

She could easily imagine Christian dancing all night and remembered that if she didn't do something, she might never find out what it was like to dance with Harlequin. It was surprisingly unbearable.

She blinked away tears and tried to devise a plan. But there wasn't much to plan other than putting on the same dark grey clothes, which were now dry, and going to the mansion to find out if it was as easy to get into as Christian's lodgings. Maybe it wouldn't make any difference at all. Maybe it was downright dangerous, but she had to try. There was no shadow of a doubt. And Helena would ensure that the night was filled with eyes that would see in the dark, if there was anything at all to see.

Anna considered her attire. It had been easy enough to break into Christian's place in ordinary clothes, but if she were to sneak or climb, the current women's fashion was not ideal, no matter how many pleats she had in her skirt. She only had her flat, rubber-soled shoes from her school sportswear so at least she was able to walk silently. Perhaps she should buy something 'for her husband'?

Anna took some measurements, chose her most discreet outfit, and went to Magasin du Nord, where a friendly men's department attendant understood the difficulty in buying clothes for a man who was in hospital but would need something when he came back home in a couple of days. Did madam have his size or measurements? Yes, certainly. And she bought a grey shirt, a dark grey knitted jumper, some narrow, dark woollen trousers, a black cap, and a dark grey coat. No, she had his shoes and underwear. It was only all the rest he no longer fit into after losing so much weight. The attendant wished madam's husband a speedy recovery.

Anna went home with her new clothes, which would withstand a trip over a fence; there were no skirts to get caught, and the coat had nice big pockets both outside and inside, so you wouldn't need a handbag. Anna tried to eat her supper but had no appetite. She was tired and lay down on the bed and fell asleep. She didn't wake until two in the morning and thought it was good, as she could leave immediately while the city slept, and without leaving too early out of sheer impatience as she would otherwise most likely have done.

The door to Christian's involuntary lodging was unlocked, a padlock unlocked, a latch lifted, and two people peered in having a whispered conversation in French.

- He's asleep.

- Good. Let him be. I have no desire to ruin something so beautiful.

- You might have to.

- I don't think he knows anything. Otherwise, he would have done something long ago. As long as he doesn't see anyone here, we should be able to finish the job, and then just leave him without handcuffs at the end. We'll be long gone when he wakes up, and whatever the police might find out, it'll be too late.

- Are you sure?

- Sure enough. Get him some more food and water.

- And he won't pursue us?

- Who would he pursue? And where? I don't want to be involved in murder. That catches the police's attention in a completely different way. And he's one of their lot, which makes it personal on a whole other level. Let him sleep and then let him be.

The door was closed again, locked, and the latch put back.

Anna arrived at the mansion, where the gate was locked as expected. The house was completely dark and the street almost deserted. There was a crescent moon, mostly obscured by drifting clouds, and it was windy enough for small sounds to disappear in the rustle of the trees. When the street was empty, Anna gave the hinges a few drops of oil and climbed over the gate as close to the side as possible, hoping it wouldn't move too much and make squeaking noises. Inside, there were stables and garages and gravel paths in a garden that would be beautiful come summer. She searched for the kitchen door. The back of the house was also totally dark. There seemed to be no one in the building – or they were all asleep.

The kitchen door hinges also got a drop of oil, and fortunately, the door was only equipped with an old-fashioned lock, which could be easily picked. Anna sneaked in and closed the door neatly behind her. The house was quiet and felt empty. There was no sign of activity in the kitchen. No warm ashes in the stove, nothing set out ready for morning chores, nothing on the shelves of either porcelain or copperware. No food in the pantry.

She tiptoed into a corridor, from which there was a staircase up the side of the building. She only took a few steps at a time, listening, sniffing, and moving on very cautiously. She was lucky; it was a stone floor, and even the servant's staircase was of stone. It was a relief – stone doesn't creak.

She had to pass the bel etage; there was hardly anyone there now, and the next floor, which probably contained bedrooms and private parlours, either occupied by the owners or empty because the season had just ended. The most likely scenario was that if someone was being held captive, it would be in the attic, in the servants' quarters, if there were any left, and where there would therefore automatically be people and activity at ungodly hours, when shoes needed polishing in the middle of the night or fires needed lighting before dawn.

Anna thought of the girls she had talked to at Maycourt Manor, even though they were told to make themselves invisible if any of the gentry appeared. But Anna had gone down to the kitchen and got tea and scones from Cook, who was kind and happy and didn't mind this crazy Danish girl gaining insight into the workings of a big house. She remembered it as a giant machine running on elbow grease.

Anna climbed the stairs until she couldn't go any further, and the walls sloped. There was a grey door to the side, which had to lead into a corridor. It also got a drop of oil, and Anna hoped it wasn't locked. There should be no need for that. It wasn't and could be opened slowly enough to almost not squeak and could be closed again with a quiet click.

She stood completely still and held her breath – not a sound. She tiptoed down the corridor, listening if there was anyone there. There were paper-thin walls and doors that gaped at the bottom, so you should be able to hear everything. Suddenly, there was a sound. Someone was moving in a bed with squeaky springs and then pissing in a chamber pot. Anna was about to burst out laughing and had to put her hand over her mouth to stop the sound of a giggle. So, there was someone here. The bed creaked again, and there was a sound of metal against metal. Strange.

Anna crept down the corridor to find the source of the noise, listening at all doors to hear if there were others. Down by a door with both a latch and a padlock in addition to the usual door lock, she could hear someone pouring water into a glass and hitting the glass with the pitcher, judging by the sound of it; not enough for it to tip over, but enough for the person to curse. 'Merde!'

Anna held her breath – it sounded like Christian. Could she be that lucky on her first ever rescue mission? Not entirely, because further down the corridor, there was suddenly also a sound of someone apparently waking, probably from the sound of porcelain against glass. She stood completely still, and whoever had poured the water was also silent. There was a creaking, as if someone were turning in bed, and then a grunt. Anna waited for what felt like an eternity. After a while, there was a snoring sound.

Anna plucked up her courage and went to the door with the latch to pick the locks, even though she really didn't know if the person on the other side would be pleased or might possibly attack her. Both scenarios were equally likely, and if it was Christian, she had no idea what role he played – whether he was a villain or a victim. But right now, there was silence, so perhaps the person had fallen asleep again.

The lock was easy enough. The padlock as well. The latch got oil and could be lifted with no other sound than a faint scraping of wood against wood. It didn't provoke any reaction in the room nor in the snoring that came from further down the corridor, so she couldn't have woken anyone.

Anna oiled the hinges and opened the door very cautiously. Moonlight came in from a small window, so you could just about make out the furniture in the room and a person in evening dress, lying on the bed half covered in a thin blanket, one arm chained to a bedpost with a set of handcuffs. She didn't know if he was sleeping, but she knew it was Christian. She tiptoed to the bed and gently blew on his face to wake him up, while holding two fingers on his mouth to signal he should be quiet.

Christian woke with a start and looked bewildered at Anna, thinking he was dreaming. She took his free arm and placed his hand on the cuff around the post, so it wouldn't make any noise, while she tried to pick the lock on the one around his wrist. It was more difficult than the door lock, so it took some time.

Christian eventually got his arm free, and the handcuffs could gently slide down the bedpost and onto the mattress.

She put her finger to her lips, pointed down the corridor, and placed her hands under her head at an angle, as if she were singing Frère Jacques. Christian understood perfectly – someone was sleeping in that direction, so they had to be quiet. He took off his shoes to walk in his stockinged feet and used the blanket as a shawl. He followed Anna out into the corridor, where she closed the door, put the latch back on, and locked the padlock.

They stood still and listened. There was no change in the snoring, so they tiptoed out of the door to the stairs and closed it behind them with an almost inaudible click. They walked cautiously down the stairs and stopped along the way, listening for other sounds. There were none. It was easy to get the rest of the way and out to the gate, where Christian lifted Anna halfway over, gave her his shoes and the blanket, and then climbed the gate. He put his shoes back on and draped the blanket over his shoulders again. The night was freezing.

- You'd better come with me. I'd like an explanation, at least,

Anna said quietly, when they reached Kgs. Nytorv and Christian just nodded. He knew a lot of people who would like an explanation, and it would be both long and difficult and not necessarily believed.

He looked at Anna, who was clearly dressed for the occasion. How on earth had she found him? He thought of how easily she had entered – maybe she had entered his room just as easily and found the invitations? That was the only explanation he could come up with, even though he knew he hadn't given her the address of his boarding house. There had never been a reason.

When they were back in Anna's room, he had his suspicion confirmed. One of his invitations lay on her desk. Explanation was unavoidable. He braced himself for a solid scolding, but it didn't come. Instead, Anna threw her coat on the bed and slipped into the apartment – first to send a telegram to Helena via the phone, which simply read 'Found unharmed. Anna'. Then she went into the kitchen, cleared the dried, uneaten dinner from the tray and raided the pantry. She came back with bread, butter, sausage, lemonade, and cake. She placed it on the table and began to help herself. Christian sat opposite and ate bread and sausage in silence for maybe five minutes. Finally, Anna looked up at him.

- Tell me. From the beginning.

He recounted life at the ballet, and how the countess had come up with the idea to hire some of the male dancers as extras for the grand parties, where there were usually young women eager to dance and older men who absolutely did not want to, and since they were taught both French and good manners at the ballet, the dancers were popular and didn't stand out. He explained how for several years he had been invited to these parties and had danced with all the ladies and been well paid for the trouble.

He had invented an alias, found a Russian order at a pawnbroker, and had made a moustache from his own hair that had matched the role, so he danced like one of their own – Count de Namours. No one had the slightest interest in who he was, as long as he stuck to his dance card and didn't speak with the same lady twice, so nobody started suspecting him of showing any personal interest in any of them.

- Since I left the theatre, I've had many of these engagements. It's like being on stage again. I enjoy it. The lights, the music. Pretending to be someone I'm not. Playing a role. Fill up with music.

Christian sounded like he wanted to say more, but he didn't. He just looked longingly at nothing. Anna stared intently at him.

- And is it just dancing?

Christian was totally taken aback.

- Yes, of course. You're admitted after dinner, given a full dance card, and usually there's only one dance per lady, so everyone gets at least one dance with a gentleman who doesn't step on their toes. And to prevent rumours. Everyone keeps an eye on everyone, and you're discreetly sent home just before the party breaks up. I'm a dancer, Anna. My legs will wither if I don't dance. And here I even get paid for it. And for nothing else, I promise. Not even before I met you. When I dance, I may be a stranger to the lady, but I am no longer a stranger to myself.

Anna understood.

- But now? What happened? Did you know anything? See anything?

Christian tried to gather his thoughts and rewind his memory to the evening and the dancing.

- I drank champagne and talked to a lady, and we just stood looking around, and then I happened to look at the countess and her tiara, which suddenly reminded me of the one you showed me from Nice. And the man she was talking to resembled the picture of one of those from the 'opera cast' from Sweden. And maybe I stared too long, because the countess suddenly looked at me. But then the music started again, and I had my duties. It was the last ball of the season, so the countess came over and said thank you and handed me a glass of champagne as I was leaving, and I drank it and went to get my coat. And then I woke up in the room where you found me, where I was first tied to the bed with rope. When I woke up again, the rope had been replaced with handcuffs, and there was food – and a chamber pot. It reassured me, because I've never heard of anyone taking that much trouble for someone they intend to kill, and they could have done so long ago – and dumped me in the canal before anyone noticed. I think the countess is involved – maybe the mastermind – but she's not a murderer. I've probably just had to be put out of the way for a while. I guess she's left with that man from Nice, and they're probably long gone and by different names.

Christian looked anxiously at Anna.

- Do you believe me?

- Yes, I actually do, because I can't come up with a better explanation. But we need to think before you talk to Madsen. Otherwise, he'll have too much to ask me as well.

- I doubt the countess will report a break-in and a kidnapping of a captive, but I don't know how my landlady will take it. Did you lock the doors again?

- Yes, of course. Both in your room and the front door. But you better take this, which I used for the handcuffs, which for some reason you had in your trouser pocket – and you'll have to come up with your own explanation – about when you were caught. Did they empty your pockets?

Christian rummaged through his pockets.

- No. Both the dance card and the money are still here. And my keys.

- Add it to your key ring and explain that you managed to pick the lock yourself. And if Madsen looks at you and asks if you didn't get any help at all, let your eyes say yes, and your mouth say no, and he can't do anything, and probably won't, and I'll get a star in the book, which one day I might need to cash. And you better go home before the whole city wakes up – and especially your landlady, who will surely be relieved but also demand an explanation or at least an apology.

Anna took a few more bites of her sausage.

- Madsen was so worried about you he called me and told me he had spoken to your landlady – he even gave me your address, which was a rather unusual expression of trust, but it was wise, and without it, I wouldn't have stood a chance of finding you. Maybe that's what he hoped for. But it means your landlady probably won't settle for just 'police work' when your boss knew nothing about it. But that's your problem.

Anna smiled sweetly at Christian, who stood up, grimaced, and looked her up and down for the first time ever.

- You look quite sharp in that outfit.

- It's comfy. Honestly, I'm jealous. Especially of the pockets.

Anna got up and gave him a hug and told him to call on Helena himself before he was let out into the night, which was now turning into morning. She hoped he would make it home before his landlady woke up. At least a real key had been used in both doors before she used hers, although she might wonder how smoothly they turned on the hinges. Anna herself needed the sleep of the guilty. It turned out to be calm and dreamless and way too short. Marie's light knocking on the door to tell of breakfast came much too soon.

Christian's journey home was almost half asleep, and he wondered all the way why Anna had so promptly gone out to look for him, as if it were a matter of course, and moreover, had called on Helena without further ado. Both had reacted as quickly as they could, without even considering their own risk.

When the man arrived early in the morning with more food for Christian and discovered him gone, he nearly dropped everything on the floor. But he dared not say anything to the countess, who expected him to let the prisoner figure things out for himself the next day and therefore didn't need to be told that the prisoner had already taken care of things a little bit earlier than expected. He hurriedly arranged his own departure, leaving much sooner than planned. There was nothing to indicate how the prisoner had been freed. The handcuffs were neatly placed on the mattress – locked and empty.

At breakfast, Christian explained to his landlady that he had followed a lead that had suddenly appeared, preventing him from informing his superior officer in time, and it had taken longer than expected, but it had brought him much further in solving an important case. Unfortunately, he couldn't tell her more. She accepted his apology for missing breakfast, as it had never happened before.

At the office, he went directly to Madsen who got the same explanation as Anna about his dance engagements, which sounded plausible enough – and could be verified through the theatre, which Christian also knew, so it would be foolish to lie about them. And then there was the explanation about the tiara and the man from the 'opera cast'. Christian would go to Bugge and look through the pictures to see if it was indeed the 'count of Pierrini'.

As expected, Madsen asked if he had received any help in his escape, and Christian smiled and made the smallest possible nod while saying no. He had picked the lock himself. Madsen looked at him. For a long time.

- Good work, la Cour. I hope your luck continues. Which it probably will. You have the rest of the day off. Get some proper food and some sleep.

Christian stood up to leave. Madsen sent him a knowing smile.

- Give my regards to Miss Lendorph.

As Christian left, Madsen was thinking the same as Christian himself had done. If his captors had bothered to feed him – even give him a chamber pot – Madsen smiled at the thought and was sure there was a woman involved – the intention was to keep him away while they disappeared out of the country. If they had wanted to kill him, they could have easily done so – and got rid of him immediately. The conclusion, therefore, was that it wouldn't make any difference whether la Cour was sent to Bugge today or tomorrow, as the thieves were probably already long gone, and they had no idea who had locked him up. It was wise not to kill him – and like everything else; it showed they had a lot of experience in the business. Everyone knew the police took very personal offence if you murdered one of their own, so best to refrain, unless it was absolutely necessary. So, it hadn't been. Carstens might not know the countess – at least not as the countess of Chambord. But perhaps as someone else. La Cour would spend some time looking at pictures tomorrow. The entire 'opera cast' and then some.

There was no way around visiting Helena and providing at least something of an explanation, but Christian wasn't sure if she was up so early, so he knocked very gently on the door. Helena opened it, wearing her entirely private face. She would normally have been very annoyed being disturbed in the middle of breakfast, but Christian had seen her worse, and she had been really worried until Anna – and thanks Anna for showing that consideration – had sent the telegram that she had found him. He was allowed in and was offered a cup of coffee and some toast, which got cold before he finished eating it while trying to answer Helena's many questions – she also knew nothing about his dance appointments. The reaction was the same as Anna's – understanding and a hug on the way out. Helena had already let it be known that he was found. He could go home and sleep. Christian would have liked to talk more with Anna, but he didn't have the energy. His body expressed its absolute displeasure at being upright and still walking about. He came home, took off his hat and coat, and lay down on the bed, falling asleep immediately. He only woke up when the landlady knocked on the door to tell him dinner was ready.

15.

It was a very bleary-eyed Anna who showed up at the newsroom and struggled through the stack of newspapers to find something juicy enough for Aftenbladet while waiting for further developments in the jewel case. She absolutely had no intention of revealing her own contributions. There were some aspects she preferred not to discuss with anyone. Especially not with the police. Except Christian, of course.

She sat quietly hunched over her work so Bærentzen wouldn't be tempted to come and talk. She couldn't face it. Fortunately, Rasmussen was absent. He usually burst in and wrote like a madman, looking daggers at her, then hurried away again. The problem with him was that you never knew when. Anna cancelled her fencing in the afternoon. She was so tired, she reasoned, she'd be a risk to her partner.

She was relieved when Marie explained her parents had accepted a dinner invitation. Peace and time to think. It turned into sleep instead, while the dinner Marie had brought stood untouched on the table. She dreamt she was dancing with Christian in a grand ballroom surrounded by ladies overloaded with jewels. One of them wore a gigantic tiara shaped like a spider in a web of diamonds.

Later in the day, when Madsen read Aftenbladet and found not a single word about Christian's exploits, the ballet, the fake countess, or anything related to the case, he was absolutely certain that Miss Lendorph was involved. He was also sure that la Cour would never admit it – not to play the innocent, but because Miss Lendorph must have used methods that nice young ladies absolutely should not use – in fact, not even know about. But he never got as far as guessing that Anna had specially crafted tools for precisely the kind of methods she shouldn't know about, and which Christian politely returned a few days later, having made a copy at his father's workshop. Instead, Madsen could read about a German doctor and his wife who had gone on a honeymoon in Norway:

A Honeymoon on a Sled

A young German couple, Dr Michaelis and his wife, went on a honeymoon in Norway, which is not unusual. What is peculiar is that the journey was made on a sled. It was quite a large sled, covered with a canopy, so it all became somewhat like a tent, and the young German doctor and his wife also used the sled as a hotel. They slept in it every night out in the snow. The trip, which went from Christiania to Kongsberg, has now ended, and the couple has returned to

Germany – although the return journey was not made on the sled.

Madsen felt cheated. Miss Lendorph could normally come up with something much better than this. But she was probably tired.

He wasn't any more enthusiastic about the article next to it, which told that Bernhardt Larsen from the World Patent Bureau planned to sell advertising space on the clouds, as he had successfully tested the method. He had received 90 amperes of electricity from Skovshoved Electricity Works for one of the army's projectors, and the experiment had been a success.

Madsen thought maybe you should start by projecting 'confess your sins' on a well chosen thundercloud to measure the effect on the audience. As expected, there was no report of a break-in at the mansion.

Christian arrived the next day as punctually as usual and went straight to Bugge's, where he received the 'opera cast' files with photos, descriptions, and fingerprints to go through.

- It might be this one – Antoine Pescanti. The countess called him Conte Pierrini, and the description fits. Short guy, brown hair, very dark eyes, pale, straight nose, high forehead. Looks like Augusto Darvia, but with slightly longer hair. Combed back. No one sounds like the countess. I think she's French. Her accent is Parisian upper class. Probably related to the aristocracy in some way, since she's been able to deceive them for so long. They don't usually let in strangers.

The countess had known la Cour as a dancer, but as far as Christian knew, she had never heard anything about his police work. He hadn't said anything – they didn't talk much anyway – he didn't know any of the others, and the ladies never asked. She didn't have his address. Whether others had recognised him, he didn't know. But they had taken his moustache. He had no idea when he had collapsed or where, so maybe it had just come off when he fell? There was no way of knowing and certainly no one to ask.

Bugge and Christian agreed that there was hardly any chance of catching them, and since it couldn't be proven that they had committed crimes in Denmark, their arrest in another country wouldn't help. Christian hadn't seen or heard anyone when he was captured, so he had no idea who it was. The only bright spot was that if they had accomplices in Denmark, it was probably

Carstens. They had Samuel and Bernhard most likely felt safer staying in England, which meant there was no further immediate danger to Christian. Whoever had wanted to flee had obviously fled so hopefully no one left.

Bugge was burning to ask Christian how he got out, but Madsen had said he shouldn't. Madsen had made sure an officer had been put on guard at the mansion, but it was completely empty. Apparently, the property had just been sold.

Christian sat lost in thought, and Bugge fetched him a fresh cup of coffee and left him alone. After 10-15 minutes, he looked up and asked for things from waiter Hansen's lodgings. Bugge brought a box, including the rings still in the cloth they had been found in. The cloth was a dirty piece of torn cotton, possibly once a large handkerchief. He picked it up and sniffed it. Then he took the passport out of the envelope it had been put in and sniffed again. He returned to the cloth.

- Do we have anything from Inger's room?

- We have her stockings. She was buried in her only dress.

- Hand them over, will you?

Bugge found the box and gave it to Christian, who sniffed the stockings. And then the cloth again.

- Try sticking your nose in these two, Bugge, and tell me what you think. Cloth first.

Bugge grimaced but sniffed the cloth with the rings and then the stockings.

- They smell surprisingly similar, except for some extra perfume-like scent on the cloth.

- Exactly. I think Inger stole the rings from Hansen and took them home and hid them in the handkerchief under the floorboards. And Hansen went there and found them and took them home and hid them at his own place. I'm sure they met each other, and the only explanation I can come up with is if Inger had stolen something from him. Maybe he was walking around with the rings in his pocket, fearing we would search his room? And maybe she tried to sell them back to him instead of going to a pawnshop, where it would attract attention. No one would ever believe she owned them.

- Sounds plausible. And then he followed her at some point to see where she lived?

- Yes. Whether he came while she was at home, I dare not guess – maybe, maybe not. But he knew the trick with the floorboard himself, so he could have tried all her hiding places – there certainly weren't any other there except the food bag, and that was gone, and the bed had clearly been moved and the mattress cut open. So, probably not at home, and he found the things himself. If she was there, why cut the mattress? Unless, of course, she was too drunk to talk.

Bugge looked at Christian. The explanation made sense – also that Hansen would do anything to get the compromising rings back. Inger could explain they were his. No lack of motive.

- The question is whether Hansen killed Inger, or her sailor boyfriend came home and saw Hansen there and killed her in a jealous rage. And he could have done that without being too out of it to think of hiding her. We need to find the sailor. And I need to get hold of Haack. There are plenty more questions for Hansen.

Christian left Bugge and went down to the harbour, continuing all the way to the Freeport looking at the many ships and the bustle of people and thought that it would be a miracle to find Peter, and that someone could long since have warned him, making him flee. At least he couldn't visit his regular watering hole in Copenhagen without Christian hearing about it.

The experience of Christian's abduction had given Anna an even greater desire to be a detective, but had also reminded her it could be dangerous. She hoped Helena would soon get hold of the Webley she had promised. The Schouboe could fit in one of the huge pockets of the gentleman's coat but not in any of Anna's normal clothes nor in a fashionable handbag, and she had a feeling that even if she didn't exactly need it, she would at least feel better equipped to face all eventualities if she were armed.

She didn't have the impression of being in direct danger herself, but if someone had followed Christian for a while, they would also know her address. However, it didn't seem likely since he was picked up on their home turf and even kept there. And they wrote to him via a post office box... Which could of course be his idea considering the name on the envelope.

Anna also decided that it was time to find a more challenging hobby than fencing, which nowadays was a tame affair and not something La Maupin would have taken even remotely seriously. Something better was needed. The question was what and how, before Christian had to catch her in the act of doing something illegal out of sheer boredom. When the jewel case was solved, and all the fun was over, it was necessary to have something else at the ready. She would love to continue the detective work – there was just no likelihood of that happening.

16.

The la Cours' grand apartment was ready for guests; delicate ornaments were tucked away, the carpet in the largest salon was rolled up and placed in the service corridor, buffets were stocked with all sorts of delicacies; beer, champagne, punch, and other drinks were chilled; chairs were lined up along the walls, extra staff had been called in, and taxis were booked for likely times of departure.

Professor Lendorph, Dr Lendorph and Miss Anna Lendorph arrived with high expectations and were greeted by a herald, who then announced the presence of Zeus, Hera, and Columbine. Just moments later, La Chatte Noire arrived, whom Anna recognised as Helena despite the mask. So, she had chosen not to be the beautiful Helen, which would hardly have required a costume, but instead a cat, so she could wear a mask covering about half of her face. Extremely diplomatic, thought Anna – and surely Mrs la Cour also, who welcomed them all with a huge grin and ushered them on to a sideboard and a drinks maestro. It boded well.

Dr Lendorph wasted no time in capturing the hostess to tell her about the collaboration with Helena, who was called upon, and the three ladies managed – albeit briefly – to agree on further dissemination of knowledge about family planning not only to maids but also to dancing girls, theatre staff, and whoever else of their acquaintance could benefit from this knowledge.

Harlequin took a beeline for his Columbine and refused to leave her for the rest of the evening, except for two dances – one with his mother and one with Helena – and a few calls of nature. Then he waited politely outside the door. Or vice versa.

Anna and Christian were, as everyone noted, a very handsome couple. Columbine looked amazing, and she had good legs. Harlequin was as beautiful as a Greek statue, it could be observed, as the costume was a silk bodysuit and therefore fit like a glove – in fact, it was sewn on. However, he would need a much larger fig leaf than the statues she had seen in the Vatican, Anna mused – as did the other women and a couple of the gentlemen in the company, judging by their glances. Some spent the evening keeping an eye on Harlequin's enthusiasm for his chosen one, but were disappointed. Many years in the theatre in close contact with women had ensured Christian's absolute control of his body. And they weren't lovers, he reminded himself. He didn't care what the others thought. They certainly did.

There was drinking, dancing, courting, performing and a lot of laughter. Anna found out what the seven veils dance could have looked like, Zeus reminisced about his encounter with Leda, making people roar with laughter, and Hera contributed by punishing him for the affair – to even more laughter. Ida had been right – the Lendorphs fit perfectly into the company and would become regulars at the parties.

Harlequin managed to detach himself enough from his Columbine to dance with the black cat, causing some to suddenly develop doubts about Columbine. But she just smiled over a cocktail and danced with a Tyrolean farmer in lederhosen, who gave a cheerful yodel, while his wife swung the large beer steins and showed she could do the splits, even carrying four litres of foaming beer.

La Chatte Noire received admiring glances – and some more investigative ones – but since she was as incognito as possible, there was no risk of embarrassing moments. Her contribution to the entertainment was, of course, Rossini. Duetto Buffo di due Gatti joyfully joined in by all the guests. Her meowing was irresistible, and especially the gentlemen responded with considerable enthusiasm. Helena's return to the guest list was also ensured.

What Christian didn't know was that Anna had secretly taken dance lessons and learned enough to be able to dance as Columbine, and Mrs la Cour, who never let an opportunity for a performance pass – in fact, it was the duty of all guests at the parties – had been involved and knew that Christian had danced Harlequin. So, a couple of hours into the party, while people's attention could still be caught, they signalled to each other, and Mr la Cour sat down at the piano and started playing the music they had borrowed from the theatre. Harlequin bowed to his Columbine and was amazed that Anna knew the steps, even dancing en pointe.

- How?

he asked, but only got a smile and Harlequin felt happier than he had ever been holding Columbine's hand to a thunderous applause. Anna caught a glimpse of what he had talked about from the stage and understood and was glad she had spent so much time – and it really was a lot of time – learning to dance a short pas de deux on secret visits, practising with Christian's father and a ballet school pupil. No one attended a party at la Cours' without contributing to the entertainment, and she had done so with flying colours.

Later in the evening, Ida and Christian competed in advanced legwork by kicking the hat off a Napoleon. In fact, they were so good at it, they could keep the hat over his head from each side with their feet. The enthusiasm was endless – as was the thirst. The last guest left the party a little after eight in the morning and was at risk of being arrested for disorderly conduct if it hadn't been for the quality of the singing. Aage Fønns declared to the world that all he wanted was more champagne while conducting himself with a Veuve Clicquot.

It had been a wonderful party, Anna concluded with satisfaction, when she finally got home to bed. Helena had confirmed that the promised Webley had just arrived from England and only needed to be picked up; it had been a fantastic experience dancing with Christian; she fully understood why he had become a fixture at the countess's balls – something that needed to be considered more carefully – and she had been introduced to a young, blonde actress who was crazy about flying, and they had agreed to accompany each other to Amager for the upcoming airshow. Her name was Mille, and she was learning to fly.

Anna was eager; she needed a new hobby and flying sounded just right. She also knew that she wanted to see more of Christian. Perhaps dancing was an option now that he had been so brutally let down by the countess? Columbine warmed at the thought and mentally scolded herself, as Anna still tried to resist what everyone else regarded as the most inevitable engagement since Adam and Eve. There had to be a way to get more of Christian sans fiance.

Christian stayed with his parents. He had been sewn into his costume and needed help to get out of it. He went to bed with a silk rose he had carefully picked off Columbine's costume. It smelled of Jicky. Anna had never hinted at anything resembling interest in him as a person per se – but she hadn't hesitated for a moment to try to and find him when he was abducted, and she must have spent hours learning to dance like Columbine. What was he supposed to think? His brain and his body quickly agreed that he was supposed to sleep.

17.

Before anyone had a chance to speculate further on how casually the jewel thieves apparently approached both the investigation and the publicity, an explanation of sorts appeared in the form of a letter to the editor in Social-Demokraten. Carstens in London was thoroughly offended on both his own and his brother Samuel's behalf. He vented his frustration, especially regarding assessor Haack, whom he evidently considered the biggest idiot despite the fact that it was the Ministry of Foreign Affairs that had handled the case. This – beside the claim that legal assistance couldn't be obtained in Denmark – only proved his own ignorance. Writing in such a manner clearly demonstrated the extreme arrogance of the thieves and thus also something about why the countess et al. hadn't deemed it necessary to get rid of Christian. They quite simply regarded the Danish police as just as hopelessly incompetent as the English.

At the Detective Office, several people sat with their newspapers, reading, rereading, and bursting into laughter. Madsen included. He had seen nothing like it. In his own office, Commissioner Petersen alternated between annoyance and chuckling.

In the newsroom at Aftenbladet, Bærentzen and Anna sat with their papers, rejoicing. And of course, with regret that the letter to the editor had been sent to

Social-Demokraten. The entertainment value was first class:

"It would honour me greatly if you would publish this in your paper. My name is Bernhard Carstens. I was arrested in London and accused of a burglary that took place in Copenhagen. The purpose of this letter is to draw your attention to the ignorance displayed by the Copenhagen Police regarding this case, not to mention the ruthless manner in which they seem to treat the prisoners during the investigation; I shall mention this later: first, I shall inform you of a few facts concerning the procedure that was used against me here in London. I need not go into details regarding what led to my arrest, but on the night of the 18th, two constables (from Scotland Yard) appeared at my residence and informed me that they had an arrest warrant against me at the request of Mr Haack, assessor in Copenhagen. This gentleman has been a source of amusement to the English authorities. Before taking any action in this matter, he could have examined the Extradition Act between Great Britain and Denmark. He did not do so, and consequently wasted time, and more importantly, the State's money on a case that was hopeless from the outset. The Extradition Act between these two states is indeed easy

enough to understand; it exempts English subjects, and I fall precisely into that category, as I was born in Stockton, in the county of Durham in England. I shall now mention the evidence that Mr Haack sent to the English authorities. It was a long list of allegations, but not one of these allegations was sworn. The authorities finally laughed and concluded that there was no evidence against me. My solicitors Ricketts & Son also remarked that Mr Haack's legal knowledge must be very poor, otherwise he would not have made himself such a laughingstock as he did. It took him several weeks to complete this case, despite being informed the case was hopeless. I shall then mention the way in which my brother, Samuel Carstens, has been treated. I have written several letters to Copenhagen, where he is being held, in which I asked him if he wanted a solicitor to conduct his defence; I have also written other letters containing stamps, but the Danish lawyers have kept these letters. I believe you will agree with me that it is a serious matter when an arrestee and Danish subject is prevented by the police from obtaining prompt legal assistance. I sent two letters to my brother, offering him a solicitor and money, but I have not heard from him, and I am convinced that the police have confiscated these letters. I hope that you will draw the attention of the public to these matters. I also believe that you will agree with me when I say that it is high time that the Danish police are stopped in their method of operation, not to mention the fact that it took them so long to handle this case. Thank you in advance.

Yours respectfully, B. Carstens."

Bærentzen and Anna agreed they had nothing to contribute to the comedy, but that Anna would see if, in a refined way, they could make fun of both Carstens and Social-Demokraten, who evidently didn't quite have a handle on the facts. But it was funny. Enough to keep them chuckling for a long time.

Later in the day, Madsen and Petersen discussed whether they should comment publicly and agreed that they should leave the clown alone in the ring, but possibly have someone call Social-Demokraten and suggest it might be wise to investigate the facts just a little bit before, for example, agreeing with Mr Carstens that it was too bad one couldn't get legal assistance.

Madsen and Petersen also agreed that they didn't need worry further regarding la Cour – if the thieves were this arrogant, they probably wouldn't find it worthwhile bothering him again. He was, after all – like the rest of the force – an absolute dullard. It was a relief, given the circumstances.

And if the countess of Chambord had anything to do with the thefts, it would require unusually strong evidence to do anything at all, since the entire Danish nobility had been guests at her parties. Madsen had tentatively inquired, and there was no doubt that the crème de la crème of society would take it as a personal affront if they were implicated in a crime of any sort, no matter how peripherally. It was discreetly hinted that Petersen could also risk a very strained relationship with the Chapter of the Order of Dannebrog should investigations continue in that direction. As long as there was nothing to establish as a fact that the countess had committed a crime in Denmark – and there wasn't, not even from Christian's explanations – there was no reason for any further investigations in regard to her parties and especially the guests.

Haack had also read the article – it was hard not to when colleagues came at him waving a newspaper while laughing like inmates from a madhouse. He was not thrilled but otherwise shared Madsen's and the Commissioner's view that they should leave the others to embarrass themselves without contributing further. It simply wasn't necessary.

Christian had stopped by him with new information about waiter Hansen and Inger, so there was something new to address at the next interrogation. Haack hoped Hansen was getting tired – he had certainly done what he could to achieve this, and Carstens, he was sure, was very close to a confession for both burglaries. Then the newspapers would have something more interesting to write about than nonsense from an inflated fool. He snorted in contempt.

The interrogation of Samuel Carstens in connection with the Rungwald case went as Haack had hoped. The evidence was sufficient, and Carstens had been ridiculed by the other inmates because of his brother's letter. He was, as expected, extremely sullen, and as Christian had been present, there wasn't much point in denying. He didn't know Christian hadn't been able to see but only smell him.

The interrogation of waiter Frederik Hansen took on an extra dimension with the murder of Inger. He was confronted with witnesses claiming she had visited him at the Esplanade Pavilion, and that he had been in her room. But he wasn't particularly willing to provide an explanation beyond being robbed and wanting his things back. Yes, he had found them himself, and no, she wasn't home. Additionally, he could confess to the burglary at Rungwald's, but he asserted his innocence regarding the murder of Leaning-Inger. He certainly wasn't a murderer. And that could be true; there wasn't a shred of evidence.

Haack and Christian had a coffee break after the confessions and agreed that it felt good to bring an end to this much at least, although unfortunately, it still didn't include the murder of Leaning-Inger.

- It might as well be Peter who came home, saw Hansen leaving, or could smell his vile cologne and throttled Inger from jealousy and anger. And if he wasn't completely drunk, he probably managed to drag her to the next room and wrap her in the tarp, before fleeing to Paramaribo. Sailors can find work anywhere. Maybe we should write to the seamen's chaplains – just to see if it could lead to something?

- Maybe. Try it. I hate loose ends.

- Same. That other Carstens – in England, I mean – he's quite something.

- One can only hope he feels so superior he makes mistakes. The arrogant ones usually slip up at some point.

- It's unlikely to be here.

- Doesn't matter. As long as someone nabs him. But I could almost wish it to be Scotland Yard. After having released him.

But there was still the Møinichen case.

The interrogation regarding the burglary at Møinichen's was brief. Hansen confessed, as rings with Møinichen's stamp on them had been found in his room. But he wouldn't say anything about where the jewels had gone. 'I don't know' was his consistent answer. Haack didn't believe it. Neither did anyone else.

Regarding Carstens, it was more difficult, but his clothing had been compared to the threads found in the hole, and since he was the smallest of the three, he was the most likely burglar. Some threads matched one of his jackets, but he still denied it. Carstens claimed his jacket was just an ordinary jacket, and therefore the threads could have come from someone else's, even though it was obvious it had been caught on something. The landlady from Istedgade recognised him as Smith, but that didn't help. However, help came from an unexpected quarter.

Two inmates in cell six casually told a supervising officer they knew it was the Carstens brothers – or rather two Danish-Englishmen – who had committed the burglary at Møinichen's. They were shown pictures of the Carstens brothers and confirmed it was them. They also said the jewels had been sold in London, which sounded plausible.

Finally, this was enough to get Samuel Carstens to confess, although he wouldn't tell what had happened to the jewels – or comment on his brother's part in the burglaries. There was no doubt that both Carstens brothers had been involved – this could also be seen from the correspondence found in Istedgade. It was obvious Bernhard was responsible for the planning. Unfortunately, if England wouldn't extradite Bernhard Carstens, there was nothing they could do. For now, he walked free, courtesy of Scotland Yard and a London court.

While Haack was interrogating, there was an inquiry from Vienna, where they also had questions for the brothers.

It turned out that Leaning-Inger's boyfriend, Peter, had indeed left for South America – not Paramaribo but Buenos Aires, and the stay had been rather brief. Visiting a dockside tavern, he had met a suitable girl and thus expected to arrange his lodging with her. Unfortunately, the girl was someone else's favourite, which the other party made abundantly clear – primarily through body language. Peter understood immediately and retaliated, after which a couple of the displeased party's mates showed up, and the girl fetched the police, which had been the plan all along. She received her agreed fee; Peter was asked for his, but had no money – at least not enough. He was relieved of his shoes, clothes, and fob watch and thrown in the cells, where the rats cautiously nibbled at his socks and then stayed away.

The Seamen's Church was notified – it was a standing arrangement if a Danish sailor was arrested. The Church knew it meant paying some amount, after which the detainee, who no one cared to feed, could be sent back to Denmark courtesy of the Church, and any relatives notified. It wasn't the first time a fare had been arranged with a priest, followed by a letter or a telegram to Copenhagen, depending on how quickly the priest estimated the ship would arrive. This time it was a telegram. It was a good business for the locals at the port, including the police, and the Church usually recouped its expenses from the relatives or, sometimes but rarely, the shipping company.

The next time Christian visited Anna, he noticed the foils were gone from the wall – instead, there was a painting.

- No more need for pointed arguments?

- It got too boring. I need more excitement, so I've switched hobbies.

- To what?

- Aviation.

- You can't be serious.

- I am. I went with Mille to watch Robert Svendsen fly at Kløvermarken in a Voisin biplane.

- Mille?

- Emilie Sannom. I met her at the party – the one with the veils.

Christian remembered the festivity's most scantily clad woman, who had even discarded the seven veils.

- Mother talked about her.

Anna attempted to explain:

- I write about other people's adventures. I need to have my own. And now that the jewel case is solved, there's hardly any chance for more detective work – or exciting rescue missions.

Anna looked Christian in the eyes, and he didn't know what to say because she was probably right. And that explained why she had immediately set off to rescue him – unfortunately, not the explanation he had hoped for, but the one that came closest to the truth. Besides, both she and Helena saw him as a friend and behaved like friends, and you go save your friends without hesitation if necessary. He had also taken care of Helena himself without needing to and without being the least bit in love. He had just been human. But it had been at no risk to himself, whereas Anna's adventure could have been dangerous, but did she see it that way? And did it matter – and now she wanted to fly?

Christian just sat there and said nothing, looking lost and despaired, until Anna took pity on him – and herself, if she were completely honest.

- But of course, that doesn't mean I'm no longer curious, so maybe you'll still keep me informed?

Madsen and Petersen looked at each other through swirling cigar smoke and then through the door at Christian, who was sitting at his desk.

- Promotion?

- Yes. I think so.

- Now? It's very soon.

- Why not? Is there an office available? The position is.

- Yes, Nielsen's. I deliberately waited to see how la Cour would do after hearing Jørgensen's praises. He was right. More than right.

- Shall we bring him in?

Madsen nodded and went out to fetch Christian.

- Come with me.

The Commissioner stood up when he entered the office, which was unusual.

- Sit down, la Cour. We have come to a decision based on your handling of the jewel case – and performance in general. We have decided to appoint you inspector effective as of today. There is an office available, so you can move your things immediately. What is your opinion of Anders Strøm?

- Good. He's good.

Christian was taken by surprise by both the sudden promotion and the question.

- Then I shall appoint him your sergeant. Is there anyone else you'd like?

Christian shook his head.

- No. I'll have to think about it.

- Do so. And congratulations.

Madsen smiled and shook Christian's hand, and Commissioner Petersen also looked pleased as he extended his hand for the official handshake.

- I'll get the papers done right away.

Christian went back to his desk, feeling a bit shaken, and started packing his things to carry them into his new, very own, office. It had happened very quickly. Faster than he had ever dared dream. Detective inspector la Cour.

He started stacking his books. What would Anna say? And Strømmen, who was now his assistant – and chaperone – he thought. And I even get another one. But I also get my own phone and can close the door.

Christian went into his new office. There was a large desk with shelves like a bookcase, a leather desk chair with armrests, and another chair at the desk so you could have a guest. There was a telephone, paintings on the walls, a large bookcase, and another table with room for even more case files and even two more chairs.

He didn't have much to move, so it was quickly done. Books in the bookcase, papers on the shelves by the desk, and the detective bag and case files on the table by the door. The exchange number was on the telephone, and he wrote it down in his notebook. He inaugurated the phone by calling his mother and inviting himself to dinner, but he didn't say why. And then there was just this other person he had promised to keep informed.

A couple of weeks later, Peter the sailor arrived back in Copenhagen much against his will and was met at the docks by Christian and Strømmen.

Peter's enthusiasm at the reception was negligible. He was also not particularly thrilled about being interrogated by Haack, but eventually agreed to give a statement.

Yes, he was the one who strangled Inger. They had argued about the primus stove – whether it should be lit – and Inger had threatened to call the police to have him thrown out. He knew nothing about any Hansen or any rings – or any hiding place under the floorboards. He had just become enraged and was just sober enough to attempt to conceal the murder and hadn't bothered to tidy up as he never intended to come back.

He had taken the food bag and cut the mattress to find out if Inger had been hiding money as he needed some to get away. She hadn't.

Anna received the news by phone. It felt completely wrong. She sat staring at the phone for several minutes afterwards, pondering how they would move on from this last punctuation mark in the case.

That same evening, Christian went to Schooner-Larsen's and told that Peter had returned and confessed to Inger's murder. It was no longer relevant to look out for him. There was general satisfaction that justice had been done, and Christian bought a round. 'To Leaning-Inger.'

There was still no word of what had become of Osvaldo, but for Christian, the case was now closed. It was too much to hope for catching Hans Bernhard Carstens as well.

At Claridge's in London, Mr Carson and Lady Chambers-Bowden sat enjoying afternoon tea and drew some attention by laughing all the time, so the head waiter eventually had to shush them. He wasn't very keen on it because the lady was one of the hotel's highly valued regulars. The tall, young gentleman, on the other hand, he had never seen before.

To be continued...

Facts and fiction

The jewel thefts are the plain truth – including Romeo and Julio and the rest of them, the letter to the editor, the package with letters and addresses, the burglary plans for Bogense, the safe-cracking competition in Chicago, the plantation owner with the pardoned sister, etc. – except for Leaning-Inger and Olga. It was the caretaker who caught Hansen at Rungwald's. It was Detective Constable Jessen who, in reality, was sent out to Møinichen.

The thieves' drawing of Møinichen's jewellery shop:

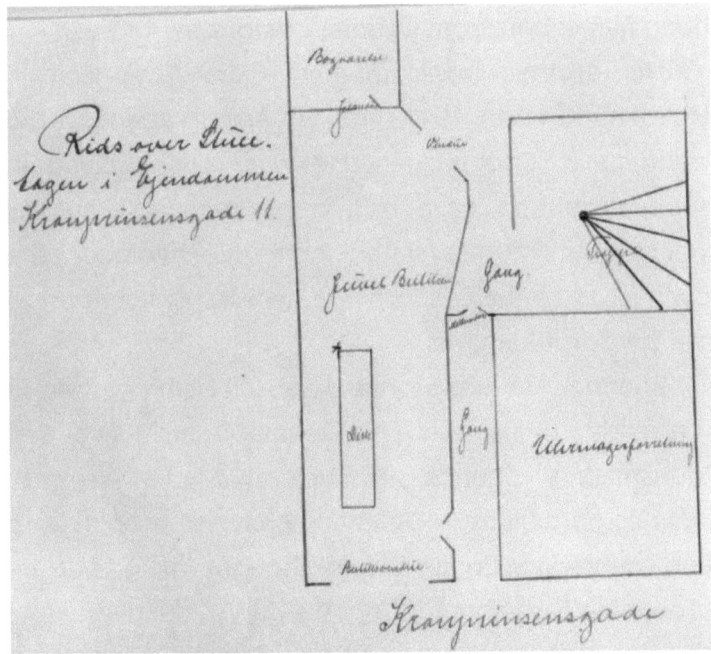

Inger's sailor was real, and he did murder his girlfriend over an argument about a primus stove and got 14 years of hard labour. But her name wasn't Inger and she had nothing to do with any jewel theft.

Monsieur Lecoq was at some point widely known in Denmark. Gaboriau's books were translated, and advertisements for the titles could be found as early as 1868. 20 years before the first Sherlock Holmes novel. Dagens Nyheder published the stories as serials from December 1868. Neither Anna nor Christian could have seen them – they weren't born yet.

Sir Arthur Conan Doyle was immensely popular already from the 1880s, and Nordisk Film made several Sherlock Holmes movies – the first in 1905. They were part of a huge film export from Denmark before the talkies.

His brother Innes married Clara Swendsen in Holmens Kirke in 1911, and Sir Arthur attended the wedding in Copenhagen. He was very involved in spiritualism and gave lectures in many places. His whereabouts are as stated in his 'Chronology'. The connection to the Lendorphs is necessarily fictitious, as the Lendorph family is.

Sherlock Holmes stories were still being written in the early 1900s even in Denmark, including Carl Muusmann's 'Sherlock Holmes at Marienlyst' with Holmes on holiday in Denmark. I haven't been able to find out what Conan Doyle thought of it, but he probably heard about it from his Danish relatives.

On stumfilm.dk, you can watch Sherlock Holmes in 'Sherlock Holmes I Bondefangerkløer' (SH in the claws of a conman) from 1910, 'Hotelmysterierne' (The hotel mysteries) from 1911 and 'Den sorte Hætte' (the black cap) also from 1911.

48,000 kr. was a lot of money – enough to buy a 6-room villa with half an acre of land in Charlottenlund (Kensington-ish) and still have money left to buy a car.

Standard fingerprint sheet anno 1910

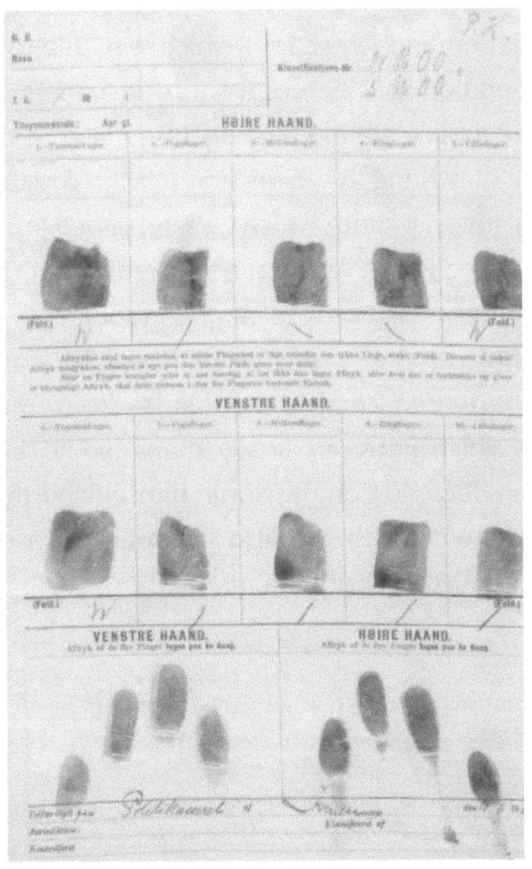

The Detective Office

was a unit under the Copenhagen police, which at that time was under the Copenhagen municipality. They were housed at the courthouse on Nytorv. The unit actually had various departments (I have chosen to merge them to not limit Christian's exploits), which dealt with serious crime – murder, arson, economic crime, etc. and functioned somewhat like Scotland Yard. The detectives were called 'opdagere' – investigators.

The detectives used Dr Hanns Gross' handbook 'Handbuch für Untersuchungsrichter' (Criminal Investigation and Detection) which was published in a Danish edition in 1899, but police inspector, chief at Nørrebro police station, Hakon Jørgensen, was in the process of writing his own handbook 'The Study of Criminal Investigation', which was published in 1912. He taught at the Police Association's evening courses, and subsequently also wrote a handbook on coding fingerprints so they could be telegraphed around the world. Jørgensen became the first leader of the Police School, which Petersen finally managed to establish, and even become Commissioner himself shortly before his premature death. He also introduced police dogs and – of course – wrote the manual.

The police gazette

was called 'Politiefterretninger' and was circulated within the police and sometimes in special editions to hotels, pawnbrokers etc. as well. It announced people apprehended, crimes committed, stolen goods etc.

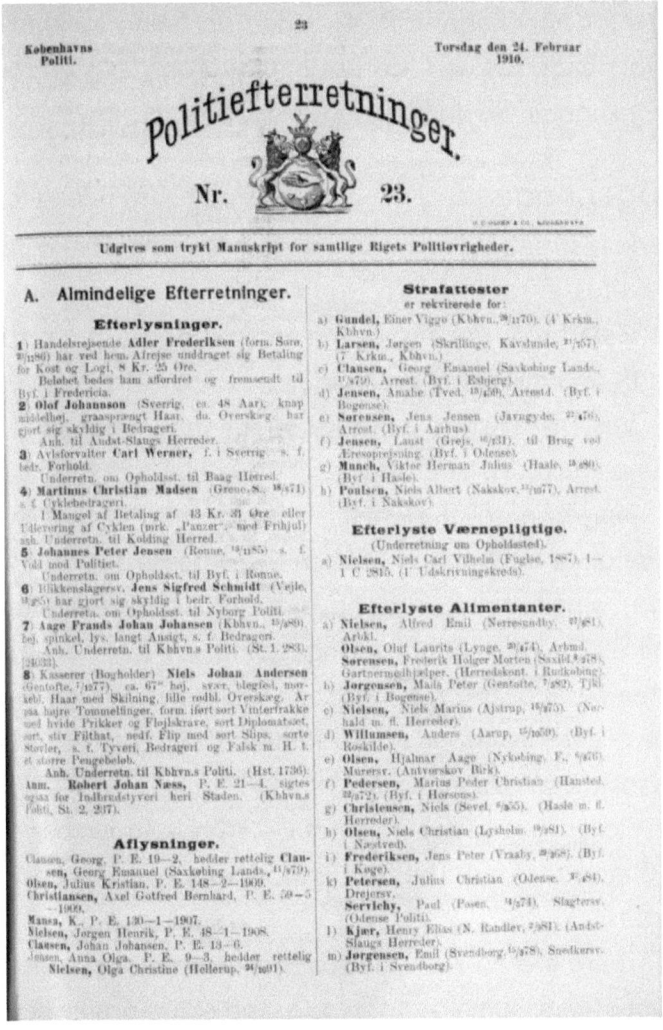

The Central Bureau of Identification

was recently established to handle evidence of all kinds including fingerprints, which were routine to use at this time.

In 1912, a joint European bureau for identification was established, which, out of respect for the efficiency of the Copenhagen office, ended up being located in Copenhagen as well. Unfortunately, it only existed for a very short while due to the first world war.

Copenhagen

Gade is street. Vej is road. Stræde is lane. Plads and Torv is a square.

Østerbro is not east as the name suggests but rather north and much posher than

Vesterbro which is more south than west (as the name indicates). A bit like

Nørrebro to the west – not north – which was developed later and in 1910 in the process of changing from small houses to housing blocks for workers. There's more manufacturing going on here than in other parts of the city. Christian was born and grew up there, and his father's once joinery shop now furniture factory is still there.

Hellerup is to the north of Østerbro and further out is Charlottenlund. The further north you go, the posher it gets.

There are no real ghettos. Some streets are poorer than others, some quarters too, and some preferred by certain groups of society but all areas kept a mixed population.

The Lendorphs live in Kronprinsessegade, a street running alongside Kongens Have (the king's garden) surrounding Rosenborg castle. It is like many streets a mix of posh flats and ordinary flats and often with businesses in the basement and the back yard. It's the very edge of 'the city'.

Anna's articles

are all from the Danish evening newspaper 'Aftenbladet' (1887-1959) 1910 issues, illustrations included. Aftenbladet has been digitized along with other Danish papers and you can read them online. Text and images long past their copyright.

Bernhardt Larsen from the World Patent Bureau did actually offer advertising on clouds in 1910. It was in the paper.

Illustrations

Images not from Aftenbladet are my own scans or photos from the original casefiles at the Danish National Archive.

English articles

The English newspaper articles referred to are real and mention the burglary at Needes. They were in the case files at the National Archives with the correspondence between court and consulate.

Main characters

Anna Elizabeth Catherine Lendorph

Born on April 3, 1882, MA (BSc) in chemistry from University College, London – foreign correspondent for Aftenbladet. Like her mother, she is emancipated and a member of the Danish Women's Society.

Tall, pretty, red-haired, fiercely intelligent, and with a twinkle in her eye. Wears Trilby hats and tailored suits in modern cuts.

Anna attended boarding schools in England and Switzerland, where she was a favourite confidante because she never gossiped and was willing to engage in a bit of assorted mischief (she still has her school fob of lockpicks).

She is related to Arthur Conan Doyle through her grandmother. This family connection played a role in her employment at Aftenbladet. Fictional.

Christian Erik Francesco la Cour

Born on October 14, 1880, his father's family of French Huguenot descent, his mother of Italian heritage. Tall, black hair, brown eyes, intelligent, extremely handsome, and trustworthy. He has a graceful posture and elegant movements – walks like a panther and dances like a god.

He was a principal dancer at the Royal Ballet but sustained an injury and had to leave the ballet. He keeps fit by continuing his ballet exercises. His theatre years also gives him a knack for reading movements and the ability to go undercover.

He grew up as a ballet child in Nørrebro, so he knows all about bullying and fought his way out of it by being able to fight until he gained respect and was left alone. He cannot ride a bicycle – he has actually never tried. Fictional.

Agnes and William Lendorph

Anna's mother Agnes Lendorph – doctor, women's rights advocate (provides information on contraception at her clinic – sales and use are entirely legal), sociable, with a dark sense of humour inclined towards sarcasm, supports her daughter in everything. Wears reform dresses. Is impatient to get Anna engaged. Born into the English aristocracy, which she left because she found them to be boring snobs. She has always been independent and was the 'deviant' of her generation. The women in the family have always had one per generation and ensured they could follow their instincts.

Anna's father William Lendorph – physics professor – taught Niels Bohr, somewhat absent-minded, agrees with his wife regarding women's emancipation, a music enthusiast for new classical music, enjoys theatre – everything from opera to vaudeville, sociable, mingling with the academic elite. The couple has regular seats at the Royal Theatre but also enjoys visiting the Frederiksberg theatres.

Both are part of Copenhagen intelligentsia. Both fictional.

Ida and Erik la Cour

Christian's mother Ida la Cour (nee Categna – from an Italian circus family and a Catholic) – former ballerina and chorus dancer at various theatres. Festive type, very outspoken, salty language, can still do splits and high kicks. Always ready with a quick remark – much more intelligent than she appears. Continued to dance when Christian was little.

Christian's father Erik la Cour – once had a joinery shop now a furniture factory and very meticulous and skilled with his business. Takes special care of the apprentices. Loves his wife. Loves theatre (where he met her), musicals, and vaudeville. Can sing and play the piano himself. Does not drink on a daily basis but enjoys a cigar after dinner. Fond of parties. He and Ida know everyone in the entertainment industry. Member of the Reformed Church like Christian. Couldn't care less about others' opinions about anything.

The couple hosts famous and fabulous parties. Both fictional.

Anders Pedersen Strøm (Strømmen)

25, big and calm, fresh from the Jutland soil. Seems slow, but perceives much more than he lets on and is definitely not dumb – rather the opposite. Good at chatting with suspects, so they confide in him. Two meters tall and broad as a door. Assistant to Christian.

Enjoys rowing and boxing and has the physique of Hercules. Fictional.

Helena Wittgens

26, beautiful, blonde, slender, intelligent, streetwise, a prostitute, Christian's friend who has upgraded from slum to luxury. He's never been a client but once saved her from being strangled, and she keeps her ears to the ground for him. They occasionally meet for a bit of gossip. She used to run a brothel when it was legal and is now independent with wealthy clients and importing and selling 'intimate articles', including through Agnes Lendorph's women's clinic. Also willing to participate in a bit of private investigation with Anna, whom she met at a lecture at the Danish Women's Society. Daughter of a prostitute who died of TB. Father unknown. Fictional.

C.W. Bærentzen

Editor and owner of Aftenbladet (The Evening Post). Former freelance crime reporter, fond of wine, women, song, and food. Fond of Anna – they share an interest in Sherlock Holmes, among other things. Slightly envious of Anna for being related to Conan Doyle. Quite okay with emancipated women – they're more fun. The biggest man in the newspaper world at 1.99 meters and 150 kg. His obesity was his downfall at the age of 47. A real person with a real newspaper. The articles quoted in the books are from Aftenbladet which is long since extinct.

Henrik Madsen

Assistant Commissioner of Police, and head of the Detective Office. Christian's boss. 55 years old, tall, slim, narrow face, moustache, cropped hair. Skilled. Known for finding talented individuals and ensuring their promotion and further development. Deeply respected real person.

Eugen Petersen

Commissioner of Police. 63 years old, still quite red-haired with a handlebar moustache, piercing blue eyes, and a very officer-like appearance. Straightforward and intelligent, caring towards his employees. Fought for more staff and an authorised police education, where the officers got paid while studying. Some call him reactionary, but that's not my impression. Real person.

J.N. Bugge

First manager of the Central Bureau of Identification – a real person in a very modern institution. Commanded great respect and with good reason. Rather young for the job, but lived up to expectations. Some called him 'the lieutenant' as he came from the military. Real person.

Carstens Brothers – Bernhard and Samuel

Brothers in crime, Samuel currently in prison for just that. Bernhard previously had a career in, among other places, Chicago as a professional and entirely legitimate safe cracker using dynamite. Real.

This photo is from the police files at the National Archives. The actual one found at Vesterbrogade.

The Countess of Chambord

Queen of the social season. Throws formidable balls. Christian's former employer as a dancer. Suspected swindler and probably major fence. Fictional.

Waiter Frederik Hansen

Waiter at the Esplanade Pavilion, convicted criminal with a penchant for diamond rings. Real person.

Mrs Berg

Preacher's widow, landlady of Christian's boarding house on the corner of Vestergade (city centre), with strict rules for the lodgers' behaviour. Very happy to have Christian as a lodger. Fictional.

Schooner-Larsen

Owner of a small dive/shebeen in a backyard near Adelgade (notorious district long since demolished), which Christian occasionally frequents to talk to various characters like Osvaldo, Olga, etc. Knows the city's underworld intimately. An acquaintance of Helena from her early days. Fictional.

Olga

A regular customer at Schooner-Larsen's.
Washerwoman/flowergirl/pickpocket/prostitute. Friend of Leaning-Inger. Fictional.

Osvaldo

Copenhagen hustler and small-time crook a la carte. Middle-aged, travels around – also in the Nordic countries – several times arrested for vagrancy in Stockholm, occasional informant to the police, so mostly left alone in Copenhagen. Regular customer at

Schooner-Larsen's. A real person who appears in police records, including the arrests in Stockholm.

Leaning-Inger
Pauper, married to a sailor, murder victim. Friend of Olga.
She got her name from a tendency to be very drunk and lean on people, until they gave her money or booze. Physically lean on them. Mostly she just got beat up. Half and half fictional and real. The murder is real but her name and other circumstances are not.